"One thing at a time, Jeanie."

Jeanie lifted her head. A streak of tears cut down from her other eye. She stared, not even bothering to wipe her cheeks. "One thing at a time?" Her vulnerable expression hardened. "Okay, here's one thing. Get out." She stood.

Michael raised one hand. "Please sit. I'm not leaving. We've got to talk."

Jeanie gave a short, bitter laugh, but she sank back down. "Why? We never *talked*, not once the whole time we were married. Maybe not the whole time we *dated*. We were together what? Four years of dating and six years of marriage? Ten years in all? And we *never once talked*."

"I know. I remember. I talked, and you agreed with me. If you ever disagreed with me, I yelled until you agreed with me. It's one of a thousand things I'm trying to face and take responsibility for. I ruined our marriage, Jeanie. Now I want to fix it."

Jeanie snorted. It wasn't a sound Michael had heard from his wife in the past. She'd grown a backbone in the years he'd been gone. Good, he needed her to be tough, to hold him accountable.

"I'm not interested in fixing our marriage. You can go now."

MARY CONNEALY is an author, journalist, and teacher. She writes for three divisions of Barbour Publishing: Heartsong Presents, Barbour Trade Fiction, and Heartsong Presents Mysteries. Mary lives on a farm in Nebraska with her husband, Ivan. They have four daughters: Joslyn, Wendy, Shelly, and Katy, and one son-in-law, Aaron.

Books by Mary Connealy

HEARTSONG PRESENTS
HP744—Golden Days
HP818—Buffalo Gal
HP821—Clueless Cowboy

The Bossy Bridegroom

Mary Connealy

Heartsong Presents

I didn't know who to dedicate this book to because I was afraid they'd either think I was calling them bossy like Michael or wimpy like Jeanie. I finally decided to dedicate this to my Seeker buddies, because they're perfect and will completely understand my intentions: Janet Dean, Debby Giusti, Audra Harder, Ruthy Logan Herne, Pam Hillman, Myra Johnson, Glynna Kaye, Sandra Leesmith, Julie Lessman, Tina Russo, Cara Slaughter, Camy Tang, Missy Tippens, and Cheryl Wyatt. Check out www.seekerville.blogspot.com.

A note from the Author:
I love to hear from my readers! You may correspond with me by writing:

> **Mary Connealy**
> **Author Relations**
> **PO Box 721**
> **Uhrichsville, OH 44683**

ISBN 978-1-60260-339-4

THE BOSSY BRIDEGROOM

Our mission is to publish and distribute inspirational products offering exceptional value and biblical encouragement to the masses.

one

Jeanie Davidson believed in miracles because she believed God loved her.

And only a miracle could make anyone love her.

Exhausted after her long day, she slipped into her favorite faded blue jeans and her pink T-shirt with the buffalo on the front. The shirt made her feel close to her daughter.

She curled up in a ball on her dilapidated couch and prayed to become a person worthy of self-respect.

"Jeanie!" A fist slammed on her door.

She jumped.

"You get out here!"

Her heart thudded. She knew that voice. It had been over two years, but she still reacted the same way—fear.

The rickety wood shuddered as Michael kept pounding.

Jeanie stumbled forward, obeying by reflex. He'd had her trained to obey without question. Tripping over her own feet, she hurried to throw open the barrier and face her worst nightmare.

Michael's battering fist almost caught her in the face. He stormed in and grabbed her by both shoulders. Tall and dark, his handsome face was an unnatural shade of red. A shade she had, unfortunately, seen many times. Michael and his temper were inseparable.

"You gave our baby away?" he roared at her, lifting her onto her tiptoes. "You threw Sally out like a piece of trash?"

Jeanie had tried to be good since she found God. Tried so hard. But her old life wouldn't stop punishing her. Then she remembered that God loved her, which reminded her of all the promises she'd made to herself. "Get your hands off of me."

Michael jerked in surprise.

It surprised Jeanie, too. She'd never heard quite that tone come out of her mouth before. She hadn't known it existed.

She yanked her shoulders, and he let her go.

His surprise didn't last long. He stepped inside, swung the door to her second-floor apartment shut, and pulled an envelope out of the back pocket of his wrinkled black slacks. He had a white button-down shirt on, sleeves rolled up to his elbows. His hair was a mess, the curls he loathed sprung free. He looked as if he'd slept in his clothes and avoided a mirror— his best friend back in the day. "What is this?"

Jeanie didn't want to be shut inside with him. She wasn't afraid he'd hit her. Michael had always done his worst with words.

She glanced at the return address: Custer County Court, South Dakota. It was his final notice, sent months ago, and his time to protest was nearly past.

"I gave Sally up for adoption." She forced her voice to remain steady when her heart was breaking. "The court made a good faith effort to contact you. It's been over two years since they first sent notification. Your parental rights were terminated six months ago. You had a long time to complain."

"I never got a letter."

"I gave them your last known address as well as your parents' address."

"My parents are dead."

"Oh, well, I'm sorry to hear that." They hadn't been subtle letting her know their precious Michael had married well beneath him. "But surely the post office forwards things. . ."

"This isn't about the *mail*. This is about a mother abandoning her child."

"And a father."

Michael opened his mouth to keep up the verbal assault,

but no words came out. Maybe even he had some shame.

"Haven't you noticed your child support checks, when you got around to sending them, haven't been cashed for a long, long time?"

Michael's mouth actually shut.

Jeanie had to keep a tight grip on her inner evil child, because it gave her great satisfaction to stand up to her tyrannical husband, and she wanted to keep at it. And she shouldn't. Meeting evil with evil wasn't God's solution.

Instead, she found the courage to step toward him calmly, neither raging nor cowering. "You abandoned both of us." She jabbed him in the chest with her index finger. Okay, a little rage there. "Even when the *money* came, *you* were never with it. Don't come in here now acting like you love our little girl or care what happens to her."

Michael's hands went to his chest as if her finger was a bullet to his heart.

"You blew it. Sally's gone. We're over. I don't have to put up with you yelling at me anymore. So get out!"

"Jeanie, I—I—"

His stutter shocked her, but it was probably due to her completely unexpected backbone.

His eyes settled. Determination.

Jeanie knew he was getting over the shock.

"You're right."

What?

Michael's head dropped until his chin rested on his chest.

"I just got this letter today. At my parents' house."

"In Chicago?" That wasn't an important question, but none of this was important. Jeanie was past caring about her jerk of a husband. Too big of a jerk to even bother filing divorce papers. And she hadn't filed. She'd married him for better or for worse and proceeded to live a life of unbelievable "worse" for six years. Since she'd become a Christian, she was even more certain that her vows were eternal. If he wanted out, he'd have to initiate it.

It didn't matter anyway. She had no intention of ever being married again, to anyone, least of all Michael "The Tyrant" Davidson. So being divorced meant being free to do. . .nothing.

"I went back to close up my parents' house, and I found this letter. It made me furious." He didn't sound furious, not like two minutes ago when he'd forced his way into her home.

"Your address here in Cold Creek is on the letter, too. I got on a plane and came straight here, in a rage."

"When are you ever not in a rage?" Jeanie shook her head in disgust.

"I'm not in a rage most of the time these days. I went back to close up Mom and Dad's house. Then I was going to find you and try to salvage our family."

Jeanie reared back, far more surprised by this than by his anger. "*You were not.* I haven't even seen you for years."

"Twenty-eight months, two weeks, and three days."

"You say that like you were counting the days of our separation, as if I *matter* to you."

"It didn't matter when I did it. But now it matters." Michael ran the fingers of both hands deep into his hair. "I had to stop at my folks' house. It's been sitting empty since Mom's funeral three months ago. I hoped she had some information in the house about where you lived. Then I saw this letter, and I saw red, and I've been running on rage ever since."

"When are you ever not running on rage?"

"I'm sorry. Before I saw the letter, I had planned to find you and beg your forgiveness. Instead, I used this letter as an excuse to be angry. You're right about Sally. It's my fault, all of it. Please say you'll give me another chance."

Seconds stretched to a minute.

Michael stared at the floor.

Jeanie stared at his dark curls.

Finally, Jeanie couldn't stand the wait anymore. "Who are you, and what have you done to my husband?"

two

Michael would have beaten himself for raging at Jeanie like this—if he wasn't a newly confirmed pacifist.

He'd had this vision of coming to Jeanie a new man, a changed man, getting down on his knees and begging for forgiveness. Instead, he'd shown himself in the worst light imaginable. But who could have dreamed she'd give up Sally for adoption?

He brushed past her, still not looking her in the eye.

Jeanie. His wife. He'd loved her since they were kids. And he'd done a poor job of showing it.

"Come here, please." He sank onto her couch. It was awful, with rips in the arms and seat. Some greenish fabric with scratchy upholstery, worn and faded until it was nearly colorless. Jeanie never would have dared let his home look so shabby. He ran a hand over the tufts of escaped batting in the rounded sofa arm.

He felt, more than saw, Jeanie sink into the overstuffed chair across from him. He'd hoped she'd sit beside him, but he was a moron even to imagine it. A spindly coffee table separated them, as well as time and his miserable behavior.

"Where is Sally?" He clamped his mouth shut. He hadn't meant to start talking there.

"Buffy adopted her."

Michael looked up. Then he pulled the papers back out. "It says Wyatt and Alison Shaw."

"Buffy's name is Alison. You know that. She's married now to Wyatt Shaw. They were in a better position to make a home for Sally. After you abandoned us, Buffy took me in.

She ended up being more of a mother to Sally than I ever was. I doubt Sally even noticed when I left."

Jeanie's head dropped back against the ratty chair.

"Buffy has her?" A huge wave of relief almost made him dizzy. Buffy had always been a better person than he or Jeanie. Buffy would take good care of Sally until Michael could get her back.

Michael saw a tear trickle down Jeanie's face. It cut a trail down her cheek and cut into his heart at the same time. He'd done it, convinced his wife she was worthless. Not fit to be a mother. It was all on his shoulders.

He stared at her and remembered that girl he'd claimed when she was far too young. So pretty, so sweet, so eager to please. He'd wanted her for her looks. He'd thrived on her sweetness. He'd married her for her compliant nature. Then he'd criticized constantly the things he loved most about her.

When the baby came and he was no longer the center of her universe, he left and blamed even that on her.

And then, through the shock of his father's death and the realization of how completely lost his mother was without a tyrant to tell her when to breathe and what to think, he'd found God and understood what love was and how badly he'd failed.

He scrubbed his face with both hands, praying silently. Strength—he needed true strength not to be the tyrant he'd been raised to be. "One thing at a time, Jeanie."

Jeanie lifted her head. A streak of tears cut down from her other eye. She stared, not even bothering to wipe her cheeks. "One thing at a time?" Her vulnerable expression hardened. "Okay, here's one thing: Get out." She stood.

Michael raised one hand. "Please sit. I'm not leaving. We've got to talk."

Jeanie gave a short, bitter laugh, but she sank back down. "Why? We never *talked*, not once the whole time we were married. Maybe not the whole time we *dated*. We were together what? Four years of dating and six years of marriage? Ten years in all? And we *never once talked*."

"I know. I remember. I talked, and you agreed with me. If you ever disagreed with me, I yelled until you agreed with me. It's one of a thousand things I'm trying to face and take responsibility for. I ruined our marriage, Jeanie. Now I want to fix it."

Jeanie snorted. It wasn't a sound Michael had heard from his wife in the past. She'd grown a backbone in the years he'd been gone. Good, he needed her to be tough, to hold him accountable.

"I'm not interested in fixing our marriage. You can go now."

She grabbed the arms of her chair to stand again, and Michael erupted from the couch, rounded the coffee table, and dropped to his knees in front of her before she got to her feet.

She jerked back as if a rattlesnake had landed on her lap.

"I'm not leaving. I'm here and I'm going to stay. I've changed, Jeanie. I'm a new man. I've become a Christian, and one of the things I've learned is that I *never* loved you like I should have. I was a terrible husband, a worse father, a sinner, a complete waste of human flesh. But I've changed." And he could prove it. "I sold my business."

Jeanie gasped.

He'd finally gotten her attention. That contracting business had been the only altar he worshipped at. He'd started it right after college graduation, and he'd been gone more than home for the six years of their marriage. Well, the marriage was over ten years old, but they hadn't seen each other since Sally was just past her first birthday.

"You didn't!"

"I'm here to stay. If it takes the rest of my life, I'm going to convince you to love me again."

"Go get your company back. I'm making a life for myself here." Jeanie grabbed a handful of his hair and tipped his head back. "I'm never going to live like I did when we were together. I spent my life begging for crumbs of affection from you. I learned to say, 'I'm sorry,' like a trained poodle. I'm surprised you didn't toss me doggy biscuits when I said it. I'm done with that, Mike. I'm a Christian, too, and I've read enough of the Bible to know a husband doesn't come to his wife screaming, beating her door, scaring her to death, and then pretend he's changed. I have no intention of divorcing you. If you want that, it'll have to be your choice, but I will *never* live with you as your wife again. *Never!*"

She released his hair. Michael saw her rub her fingers together unconsciously. He remembered that she'd loved to touch his hair. She'd always been a sucker for his looks. It made him sad to realize what a shallow reason that was to love someone.

She stood, and Michael grabbed her knees, but she shook him off. "You cost me *everything*." Her voice broke, but she squared her shoulders and went on. "I gave up my daughter, my home, my heart, and—most of all—my *soul* to you. God has forgiven me for that, but I'll never forgive myself."

He heard her voice break again, but she didn't crumble. "I've lost my daughter, but I have found a home. My heart is my own. And my soul belongs to God. And to live under your thumb, I'd have to give all of that up. *I won't do it!*" She reached for the door.

Michael was upright before she could get out. He turned her around, pushed her back against the door, and leaned over her, knowing the thrill he'd always gotten from dominating her. She'd gotten a thrill from it, too. Such a messed-up excuse for a marriage.

It was sick. He was sick. A sinner.

God, God, God. Forgive me.

He released her, raised his hands, and stepped back. He looked at her, expecting that same familiar twisted pleasure at his bullying. He saw only contempt.

Shocked, he backed off another step.

Good for you, Jeanie.

She swung the door open and walked out. Once outside, she turned toward him on the landing of the outside stairway that led to the alley below. The only other way up to her apartment was through Farrens' Pharmacy on the ground floor, but she never used that.

"Are you leaving?" She crossed her arms and glared. "I won't let you drive me out of my home for long. People in this town will protect me. I've been here long enough and worked hard enough that they won't believe your lies when you tell them I'm lazy and a liar and not worthy of your *greatness*. So leave, or I'll get the sheriff and have him throw you out."

He'd blown it. He hadn't lost his temper in three months, ever since he'd made his commitment to the Lord. The peace that had washed over him had overcome all of the old demons that goaded him, and he'd thought he was healed.

You don't have to put up with that.

Satan whispered lies justifying his anger.

Your employees are stupid.

He'd believed he was superior to everyone.

She'll shape up or she'll lose me.

But those lies had faded, and God had sent comfort like warm rain, hydrating the cracked soil of his heart, drenching the raging fire of his arrogance.

He'd been fine. . .until today.

God had deeply convicted him of the sin of his marriage. The way he'd treated sweet, malleable, beautiful little Jeanie. The way he'd abandoned his baby girl. His rage had been healed in the instant he'd been born again, replaced with conviction of his sins and the desperate need to make things right. He'd set out to find his family with a humble heart.

And now, after a few minutes with Jeanie, that sinful nature awoke like a hungry beast. He felt controlled by his need to vent his temper and always, always blame her.

He prayed as he stepped out on the landing. "You're right again. Is there a pastor in this town that you like?"

"You won't be able to turn him against me, Mike. I've done a lot of counseling with him, and he knows me well enough not to believe your insults."

"Good, then he'll know it's all my fault and we can save a lot of time. What's his name?"

Jeanie hesitated, but there was a depth to her expression that had never been there before. Yes, she'd changed. She was stronger, more confident, and if possible, sweeter than ever. She wouldn't deny him a chance to talk with her pastor.

"He's Pastor Albert Lewis. He's in the phone book." She gave him a level stare as she slipped past him and stood inside her wretched apartment. "We're not saving this marriage, Michael. I've fought too hard to stand on my own two feet and live a life God might—just might—respect. I'm not letting you denigrate me until you pull me back down to the level you need in a wife."

Michael returned that level look. The moment stretched. So sweet, so submissive, so pretty. He realized with a start that she was nearly thirty but she looked like a kid. She wasn't wearing a bit of makeup, and he saw freckles scattered across her nose. He'd always harassed her about covering them with makeup.

Her hair was pulled back in a no-nonsense ponytail. It was straight and honey blond, not the flashy, permed platinum he'd goaded her into. He'd called her hair mousy brown or dishwater blond. She had lost all of her curves, as if she'd starved away her womanhood. He'd goaded her about being fat once she'd gained an hourglass figure from giving birth.

He'd been a nonstop bully, and he deserved her contempt. Deserved to be alone for the rest of his life.

God, please forgive me. Help me to make Jeanie forgive me.

She looked like the girl he'd fallen in love with. His Jeanie. Before he started "fixing" her.

Tears burned his eyes, and he blinked, not wanting her to give an inch. He knew the kindness of her heart. She might give him another chance just because he cried, and he didn't want that.

Not when he'd just discovered it was within his power to destroy God's miraculous healing of his temper.

"I'll go talk to him. But I'm not leaving town. I'm here to stay. I love you, sweetheart, and we are going to heal this marriage. I promise you that before God."

He turned and trotted down the squeaking, protesting iron steps.

At the bottom, he looked up and saw her leaning over the railing, staring down at him as if she were looking right into the eye of the devil himself.

He turned and jogged away from her, knowing he had only the slimmest control over his need to go back and convince her, by force if necessary, that they could be together again.

three

Her mind had chased itself around and around until she thought she'd go mad.

Jeanie rolled out of bed the next morning, grateful for the first blush of sunrise that put an end to this farce of sleeping.

She should have gone down to the Cold Creek Manor to see if the night shift needed any help. As it was, she'd be three hours early for the senior center. She didn't usually show up until eight.

Showering in the tiny bathroom, she tried to get the cobwebs to clear from her aching head.

Michael was back.

Mike.

God what can I do?

She stood in front of her miniscule bathroom mirror and stared at the scripture she'd claimed for a life verse. It was taped there as a reminder to start her day with God. Taped there to remind her that strength had never come easy. Quitting, depending, and blaming were more her style—along with living with shame.

"We want you to be very strong, in keeping with his glorious power. We want you to be patient. Never give up. Be joyful" (Colossians 1:11).

Pulling on khaki slacks, white sneakers, and a light blue cotton sweater because the kitchen at the Golden Days Senior Center was always cold, she spent a quiet time with her Bible, searching for new verses about being strong in the Lord. She studied ones she knew and made notes when she found another one. She'd been doing that since she accepted the Lord.

She prayed and claimed that strength. When she felt in control of her roiling emotions—something that would probably last only until she saw Mike again—she left her apartment. As she descended the stairs, she continued to reach with her soul for communion with God.

"We want you to be strong."

God, please make me strong.

"Never give up."

That's what Michael makes me want to do. Give up.

"Be joyful."

That one she could never manage. Oh, she was happy enough. She enjoyed her work and the friendly people in Cold Creek. And she felt joy in the Lord. But she never felt joy deep inside where she knew she'd failed at her most fundamental calling—motherhood.

She could feel her will slipping. She had it in her to be a doormat. She wanted it. Letting a man be in charge meant she had no responsibility. In exchange, she had to allow herself to be demeaned night and day for her whole life. And that was easy. She'd learned it at her father's knee.

Jeanie's father and Michael's father were matching tyrants. Their mothers—perpetual victims. Jeanie and Michael had created a home exactly like the ones they'd been raised in.

Jeanie quickened her pace, trying to escape her thoughts, until she was running the two blocks to the Golden Days Senior Center. But she couldn't outrun her mind.

Once inside, she fought to regain her calm. She was so early she could bake bread in plenty of time for lunch. There were twenty-five people who came to eat, a wonderful group of elderly who treated her as if she were their own daughter. That meant they meddled and nagged and gave her endless advice. But it was all done with love. And she'd never felt such love before.

Except from Buffy. Her little sister had tried to love her.

And Sally. Her daughter had endless, unconditional love to give, but Jeanie had thrown away what Sally so innocently offered.

Neglecting Sally, rejecting her daughter's love, then giving her up was a sin for which Jeanie couldn't forgive herself. No matter how fully God had forgiven her.

She began her busy day by slipping a roast into a slow cooker and adding seasoning. She usually baked the meat in the oven, but it wasn't yet 5:00 a.m. There would be plenty of time for it to cook. Her seniors would enjoy the especially tender meat.

This was Monday. She usually got here close to 8:00, got dinner started, then ducked out just before 9:00 to help with Peaceful Mountain's church service at the Cold Creek nursing home. Then she came back to the senior center and worked until 1:00. Next she went to her second part-time job as a nurse's aid at the nursing home. She was training to be an LPN through a program at the nursing home, and she was enjoying that.

Well, she didn't enjoy the textbooks. She'd never been good at her studies. Her grades were good, but she had to work hard to keep them up. Nevertheless, the hands-on work was an easy fit, and she felt a wonderful sense of accomplishment.

Jeanie spent her supper hour as a hospice volunteer. She currently had two patients at the manor whom she was helping escort into the next life with dignity, offering support to distraught families. Working with these families instead of eating had shaved twenty pounds off her overly round frame.

She had Bible study on Tuesdays and choir practice on Wednesdays. On Thursday evenings she worked her third part-time job, four hours at the Cold Creek library. She led a 4-H Club on one Saturday morning a month, helped with Girl Scouts the next week, and filled in at the local mini-mart the third and fourth Saturdays, for her fourth part-time job.

Saturday afternoons Pastor Bert gave her a ride out to the Peaceful Mountain Church she attended. She practiced the piano for Sunday services. It had taken hard work to remember those rusty lessons from childhood, but she was good enough now to play for church. After she practiced, she cleaned the little clapboard country church, mowed the lawn, and tended the flower beds when needed.

She still didn't do enough to make up for abandoning her daughter.

Kneading bread in the empty kitchen at the run-down senior center, she prayed, trying to get her mind to settle down so she could think.

"Hi, Jeanie."

A scream ripped out of her throat. She jumped and knocked the huge circle of dough sideways.

Mike snagged it in midair. He'd always been good in an emergency. Quickly, he set the dough back in front of her.

Heart hammering, she waited for the cutting remark.

Clumsy, jumpy, nervous, daydreamer, stupid, stupid, stupid.

"I'm sorry I scared you. I went by your apartment and you were gone. Pastor Lewis said you work here mornings."

Jeanie snapped, "What were you coming by for? I told you to stay away from me." Suddenly, kneading the bread was a perfect excuse to take out her frustrations. She turned all of her anger loose on the defenseless loaf.

Mike turned and leaned his back against the counter. He crossed his arms and ankles and looked at her.

She glanced up and saw his eyes shift to the pummeled dough. It was possible he got the message.

"I know you, Jeanie. Even if I never gave you any respect, I had to know you really well or I wouldn't have been able to hurt you like I did."

Jeanie's hands stopped in mid-punch. "What?"

Their eyes locked.

"I knew you doubted that you were smart, because Buffy was such a genius. I knew how your dad went for your intelligence when he wanted to hurt you. I knew that drew blood and you'd never defend yourself."

She couldn't look away. She'd never demanded respect. Never figured she deserved it. Now here he was admitting it. In effect handing her his best weapon.

"I knew you based every bit of your shaky self-esteem on your personality and looks. You were so popular and pretty and you worked so hard at both. I wanted it for myself. And once I had it—had you—I set out to take that bit of confidence away from you."

"Go away, please." Jeanie tore the huge, smooth circle of dough into three equal pieces and began forming loaves. Her hands worked automatically. She'd done this a hundred times in the six months she'd worked at the center. Twenty-five people for lunch, each loaf fed about twelve. Crust pieces were hard to chew, so that took away six.

Michael's right hand settled on her shoulder, and she couldn't ignore him anymore.

She narrowed her eyes at him, doing her best imitation of a woman with courage. "Oh, are you still here?" She held his gaze.

"I talked to Pastor Lewis last night for about two hours."

Jeanie gasped. "It was already late when you left my place."

"I was too desperate to wait."

"Too impatient, you mean."

Mike shook his head. "I was awful to you last night. I had all these plans about proving to you that I'd changed, and then I just fell right back into the same old habits. But that was one night. I went straight to talk to the pastor. I was clear about our breakup being all my fault. He agreed to be a marriage counselor for us." Michael grabbed the receiver of the black wall phone and punched in numbers while Jeanie tried to process what he'd said.

"Marriage counseling? No, we're not doing that. We're through."

"Hello, Pastor Bert? It's Michael. I'm at the senior center with Jeanie right now."

"Michael, hang up that phone!"

Michael obeyed her, which threw Jeanie for a loop.

"He was on his way to town for coffee anyway. He'll be here in about five minutes."

Jeanie resisted the urge to smash one of her lovely loaves right in his face.

Michael seemed to sense the direction of her thoughts. That didn't make him a genius. It wasn't as if she was trying to hide her rage, after all.

"So, do you work all morning to get the noon meal ready, or do you have a break?"

The nerve of the man almost choked her. "Are you serious about trying to breathe life back into our marriage?"

"Yes, absolutely." Michael came up to face her.

She turned and nestled each spongy dough ball in the greased loaf pans. "Then you're doing it just exactly wrong by forcing your way into my life and dictating that we'll go to marriage counseling. How am I supposed to think anything but that you're the same tyrant you always were?"

"So, if I'm doing it the wrong way, then there must be a right way. So you're saying we can fix this marriage."

"I'm saying get out. I've said that any number of times, but as usual you're calling the shots." Relentless jerk. That's how he'd convinced her to marry him right out of high school. He'd been a senior when he'd asked her out at the end of her freshman year. All through college he'd pressured her—in every way.

He'd pursued her, loved her, flattered her. She'd been thrilled and honored, and when he criticized, she'd twisted herself into a pretzel to make him proud.

"I'm not interested in healing this relationship. I'm finally learning to respect myself." Well, she intended to learn. . .someday. No luck yet.

"You told me you don't want a divorce." Michael-the-Deaf-Man settled on a chair at the rectangular kitchen table and scooted another chair out a bit. For her. She considered using it on his head.

She set the loaves in a sunny window, covering them with a dish towel to rise. It chafed that Michael was exactly right about one thing. She had nothing to do for about two hours.

She perhaps should speak a little louder. "Get out, Michael. We've got nothing to discuss. Unless you want to start divorce proceedings. I'm not going to do it, but I will go along with it if you wish. I made my vows before God, and I intend to keep them."

"I agree. We took vows, and they're eternal. Our marriage is for life. Sit down."

More orders. He was trying to be nice, and he still couldn't stop.

"That's wonderful." Hands clapped together in glee.

Jeanie jumped. The hardy voice turned her around.

"If you've got a good grasp of God's plan for marriage, you can make this work." Pastor Lewis was here. And he'd gotten just exactly the wrong message.

Michael stood and extended a hand to Jeanie's pastor. The two greeted each other like old friends. They back-slapped and smiled, and Jeanie felt it happening. Already she was being pushed aside, the submissive wife, the troublemaker who didn't want to fix her marriage. She washed her hands, trying to figure a way out of this trap.

"Pastor, we talked about this last night, but I want to repeat it in front of Jeanie, with you as a witness. I abandoned her and our daughter. I take full responsibility for the mess we're in. The reason I want you here is because I'm a tyrant, unkind, unloving. I've found Jesus since we broke up, and I'm here to try to make up for all I've done."

Jeanie felt like she was hearing words that she'd only imagined in her wildest dreams. Hanging up a hand towel, she shook her head a bit, trying to make sense of what he'd said.

"I thought I could come here and make things right." Michael shoved his fingers into his hair just as he had last night. Acting agitated, unsure—it was a completely foreign gesture. "But the first words out of my mouth were said in anger. Then later I started bullying her and, worse yet, enjoying it. I don't think we can handle it without professional help."

Michael turned to her. "I'm sorry about last night. When I was born again, I felt the anger lift off of my heart and I thought I was healed. But yesterday I found out it's still there, dormant for a while but still close at hand. I've got a long way to go, and even if you promised to be strong and keep me accountable, I'm afraid we'd slip right back into the same patterns. That's why I want the pastor involved."

He said it like their marriage was fixed. Like they were only working out details.

Tears burned at her eyes.

Pastor Lewis, a rotund man, tall and full of gruff kindness, rested one of his huge, gentle hands on her arm. "Sit down, Jeanie. I told Michael that you and I have talked about your fears many times and the pain of your marriage and giving Sally up. I understand how hard you've struggled. I just want us to talk together for a while and see if we can find a starting place. I don't expect a few minutes of talk to settle years of strife."

Jeanie looked from the pastor's red-cheeked face to Mike's chiseled, tanned profile. Both of them were strong men. She knew Pastor Lewis was her friend and a wise counselor. But he was trying to bend her to his will just like Michael did.

Or maybe he just thought this was the right thing to do.

She sank into the chair Pastor Bert pulled out. Michael, straight across the small table while the pastor sat on the end between them, reached out to clasp her hands as if she'd just declared her undying love and agreed to forgive him everything.

She moved to shake his grip away when the pastor said, "Let's join hands and pray."

With an exhausted, tearful sigh of defeat, Jeanie let Michael hang on even as she knew his grip would pull her under and destroy her.

four

Michael fought down the triumphant sense of victory as he held Jeanie's hand.

"Jesus said we are to forgive seventy times seven," the pastor began.

Seventy times seven equaled four hundred and ninety, and Michael knew he was already way over. He'd probably needed forgiving four hundred and ninety times before their one-month anniversary.

When the prayer ended, Pastor Lewis focused on Jeanie. "You'll notice my prayer was one of forgiveness, from God and for each other. It's not just Michael who has sinned here, Jeanie. When one partner is the more dominant personality, the problem isn't just that he's calling the shots; it's that you're letting him. He gets in the habit of not listening to you, and you get in the habit of not even telling him what you want."

Pastor Bert reached in the breast pocket of his suit coat and pulled out. . .an inflatable baseball bat. "I want you to hit Michael with this every time he tries to bully you."

Jeanie lifted her head. Her shoulders squared. She jerked her hand loose from Michael's and reached for the bat. She ripped its cellophane wrapper open and began blowing it up with a vengeance.

"Uh, Pastor Bert, I've never heard of this before." Did he carry one with him at all times? How often did he recommend this technique?

The pastor ignored him and kept talking to Jeanie. "And this is just for him overruling you, being a bully, demeaning you, insisting on having his way without consulting you or

26

respecting your opinion, hurting your feelings in any way. If you ever feel like Michael is *angry* at you—we've talked in counseling about the fear you lived with. If you feel that, call me anytime, day or night. I will personally come to your place and throw him out.

"H—her place?" Michael's heart started pounding. Was the pastor going to recommend they live together? Michael wanted that so badly he was afraid to hope.

"Yes, you need time together to fix this, and I believe you can do that best together, platonically for now." Pastor Lewis's eyes narrowed, and Michael wished the man would go back to talking to Jeanie. "But if your wife calls me, even *once*, I will personally come and throw you out, at which point you will do your counseling from separate addresses. And we will begin counseling immediately. Together for now, the three of us, at least once a week. I may decide you need individual counseling as we go along. I can come here early in the morning or whenever is most convenient. I'm not leaving Jeanie to contend with you on her own."

Knowing these were rules he needed, Michael agreed quickly.

Jeanie was too busy blowing up the bat to voice what Mike was sure would be a protest.

Maybe she was looking so forward to whacking him and throwing him out, she'd actually let him move in. Then all he had to do was be perfect, and he could stay. Praying silently for God to renew the miraculous healing of his temper, Mike knew it wouldn't be easy.

God, You know I need supernatural control. Help me to be a better person. Help me to find joy in kindness. I need You to be with me every second of every day.

"And now, Michael, we're going to talk about your sinful treatment of your wife, one of the smartest, sweetest, hardest-working women I've ever known. She has a beautiful heart for the Lord, and her gift is to serve others, one of Jesus' highest callings, and you've taken advantage of that."

The pastor was off, and by the time he was done telling some hard truths, all based on Michael's own confessions of last night, Michael felt like a worm—which he was.

"True strength doesn't come from anger and domination. True strength comes from self-sacrifice and patience. Jeanie is much closer to true strength than you. You think it proves you're strong when you bully her, but it doesn't. You're a weakling."

Michael was squirming in his chair, humiliated in front of his wife.

Then the pastor turned his fire and brimstone eyes on Jeanie. "And you think he's strong and you're weak. But there's nothing weak about the woman I know. You're a child of God, a precious creation. God calls us to be humble, but true humility doesn't mean you allow denigration and abuse. It means you stand strong enough against Michael to not *allow* him to sin."

He included them both as he finished. "The point of the bat is to *remind* Michael he's off track. It's Jeanie trying to help you. She could do that as well by holding up her hand or leaving the room."

"But that wouldn't be as much fun." Jeanie clutched the bat and looked at Michael until Michael was almost afraid to move. She was just looking for an excuse to whack him.

"And it doesn't matter if you think she's wrong, if you think she's being too harsh. The whole point of this is to *hear* her, to *listen*, to respect her feelings. Right or wrong, she's entitled to voice an opinion. If she's feeling controlled, then you need to figure that out and stop whatever you're doing and apologize and shape up."

"Now, I'm going to give you an assignment to work on tonight. Write down all the things you love about each other and share those lists while you're alone."

"That won't take long."

Michael didn't remember Jeanie having such a sarcastic sense of humor.

"Now, let's pray."

When the pastor finished, he said, "Michael, you're going to spend the day with Jeanie. I know Monday is a busy day for her, and you've admitted you're unemployed."

Michael flinched. Pastor Bert made it sound as if Michael were a homeless vagrant. He'd made a fortune selling his company. With building contracts stretching out two years, there'd been a bidding war to buy it. Plus he'd inherited more from his well-to-do parents. If he was smart, he could live comfortably for the rest of his life. And Michael knew he was, indeed, very smart.

Pastor Bert glared at Michael in a way that made him feel stupid. He had to fight to keep from sliding lower in his chair. "I want you to spend the day being a witness to your wife's beautiful servant's heart. So, whatever she does today, wherever she goes, you go along."

Then the pastor turned to Jeanie. "Bring the bat."

five

She hadn't whacked him yet, but neither had she spoken to him.

Pastor Bert accompanied them to the Cold Creek Nursing Home and stayed through the first half of the Monday morning worship service. The social room of the nursing home was a brightly lit place filled with people who were, for the most part, sleeping.

"Good morning, Mrs. Tippens. How are you?" Jeanie crouched so her face was at a level Mrs. Tippens could see. The woman was so bent over in her wheelchair she had her chin resting nearly on her lap.

Michael was stunned as he watched Jeanie work the crowd. She knew all of the residents by name, had personal words for them, asked about their children and their health—even though half of them didn't react. When she'd touched nearly every shoulder, she took her place behind the piano, laying her bat on the low top of the spinet.

Michael hadn't known she could play. Maybe she couldn't when they'd been together.

He stood at the back of the sitting area with no idea what he should do. Pastor Bert stood in front of a semicircle of occupied wheelchairs and couches. He led a few hymns while Jeanie played the out-of-tune piano. Then the pastor told Jeanie and the three other women helping with the service to carry on.

On his way out of the door, the pastor stopped and patted Michael on the back. "I'll see you tomorrow at the Golden Days Senior Center at 6:00 a.m. to go over your lists."

He must be afraid to let them go two days without being observed. Smart man.

As Jeanie and her friends worked their way through the service, Michael wondered what he'd write on his list. What did he love about Jeanie? Why had he seen her and wanted her immediately?

He knew the truth was brutal. She was pretty. And she gave in to peer pressure out of a desperate hunger for approval. The second had been her most attractive trait. He prayed for God to let him take his batting like a man when he told her that.

Then it dawned on him that there was a lot more to Jeanie now than there had been then. Mainly because, without his telling her every move to make, she'd found herself and become a far more interesting person than the one he'd created.

He'd created? Michael flinched. Talk about playing God.

Michael was glad he didn't have to make a list of the things he loved about himself. Right now he wasn't sure he could come up with a single one.

After the service was wrapped up and Jeanie had taken time to tell each listener good-bye, one of the other church women—Pastor Bert had introduced her as Mrs. Herne, the mayor's wife—gave Jeanie a hug. "It's so nice to meet your husband."

Jeanie shrugged. "We've been separated. Michael wants to reconcile." She looked at him, her hand clutching the neck of her bat balloon, not even pretending they weren't talking about him. He walked over as Jeanie went on. "It's a bad idea, though. We had a terrible marriage. We're both new Christians now, but we married for all the wrong reasons, and we brought out the worst in each other."

Michael came to her side. "Hello, Mrs. Herne." He offered a hand.

The woman, about twenty years older than Jeanie, gave

him a kind smile. "It's Carolyn. I hope you two can figure things out. Remember that with God all things are possible."

Jeanie spared one testy glare at Michael. "Meaning it will take a miracle to ever make me want to be married to you again."

Michael kept a smile on his face by sheer willpower.

"We've got a funeral at church tomorrow," Mrs. Herne said.

"Yes, I heard Myra passed away."

"Would you be able to bring something? Bars or sandwiches?"

Michael opened his mouth to tell the woman Jeanie was already too busy and any spare time she had needed to be spent with him.

The bat settled on Jeanie's shoulder, and Michael didn't voice his opinion. "I'll bring bars. I'll be down to help, too, as soon as we're done with lunch at the center. Pastor Bert seems to want Michael to stay nearby for a while, so he can come along."

"Thank you." The redheaded woman split her smile between Jeanie and Michael. "We really appreciate it." She left.

A second woman came up. "I heard you talking about Myra. I knew she was failing, but I hadn't heard she'd died."

Jeanie nodded. "Late yesterday."

"We're having a planning meeting for the Memorial Day celebration tonight. We'd love to have you there."

"I'll be there. Michael, too."

Michael turned to Jeanie. "I had hoped we could spend some time together tonight."

Jeanie narrowed her eyes. "Hope all you want."

The last church woman gave Jeanie a quick hug and invited her to tea when she had a free minute. They both laughed as if they knew that would never happen.

Jeanie said a final good-bye to her sleeping congregation.

Michael had to admit several of the elder folks had sung along with the old standard hymns, and he'd been moved by that. Jeanie was doing something worthwhile.

She left the building without looking back.

Michael felt a spurt of irritation as he scrambled to keep up with her.

As Jeanie strode across the paved parking lot, swinging her bat in time to some military march music, Michael had to jog to catch up to her. They reached the street, and Jeanie turned left. There were no sidewalks in this residential section of Cold Creek, but no traffic either, so walking in the street seemed safe enough.

"Where are we going?"

Jeanie glared. "How did you end up getting Pastor Bert to let you stay with me? It's a terrible idea. The only reason I didn't fuss about it is you won't last a single night. If you have to leave as soon as you lose your temper, we won't even get through one meal." She looked forward and picked up her pace.

Michael hesitated to ask where they were going again. It didn't matter anyway. He'd just follow her wherever. "So, what's the schedule for today?"

She whacked him with the bat.

six

It had to be a sin. It felt too good.

Forgive me, God. I'll wait until he's got it coming.

That shouldn't take long.

"Jeanie, while we walk, talk to me about Sally. Please."

She turned on him, and he flinched, lifting his arms to cover his face. Oops, the tingle of joy told her she was sinning again.

"Please, I'm not going to say a word about your choices. I just want to know how she's doing."

Jeanie walked on, lengthening her stride. Of course that long-legged jerk Michael kept up easily. Sally was his daughter, even though he'd been as rotten a father as a child had ever been saddled with.

Fine.

"She's five, almost done with kindergarten. She lives out on Wyatt Shaw's ranch. *He's* her father, and he's a good man. A fifth-generation rancher. Buffy's really happy with him. They've got cattle and buffalo on the ranch, and Buffy's made a really nice tourist destination out of the buffalo. Plus they've started supplying a string of really top-flight restaurants all across the country."

Michael shoved his hands in his pockets. She could tell by his clenched jaw that he wasn't happy with her, probably because she was talking about Buffy, not Sally.

"She started half-day kindergarten last fall. She goes to Peaceful Mountain Church, and I see her every Sunday. She calls me Aunt Jeanie, and I know her really well. I babysit sometimes. Wyatt has twin sons older than Sally, and Wyatt and Buffy have a baby of their own."

"Four kids, huh?"

"Yes. Sally is really happy. She's got a great life. She doesn't know she's adopted."

"How can she not?"

"I moved in with Buffy right after you left. Sally was eighteen months old. She bonded with Buffy immediately, and I let it happen. I didn't even care that I was losing my daughter. I thought I deserved it. Sally knows I'm"—Jeanie shrugged, not sure how to put it into words—"special. We've developed a truly loving relationship. Buffy wants to tell her the truth when the time is right."

Michael nodded and didn't comment. Jeanie hated that. She really could have used an excuse to swing away. "She's blond like I was. Short for her age, but not overly. She's just beautiful, Michael. Happy, bright, she already reads a little. And she can count to one hundred with only a few numbers missing and write her name. She got your brains, praise the Lord."

"My IQ is probably high, but if they measure brains by the way you use them, then I'm an idiot, and we both know it."

Jeanie's heart twisted at Michael's words. How she'd have loved those words years ago. Now it seemed as if her heart was dead. She could fear him, she could despise him, but she just couldn't love him. Her love for him had cost her too much.

She turned up a side street lined with tall oaks. The sun was warm for spring. Rugged mountains hugged the little town. Sluggish Cold Creek, which gave the town its name, was visible between the trees on the south side of town as Jeanie led the way toward Main Street. It was a picture postcard of a town, tucked into the majestic Black Hills of South Dakota. Jeanie felt as if her peace, although it came from God, was nurtured by the beauty that surrounded her.

And with that peace came a trickle of courage. "One of the things I'd put on that list of why I loved you was *because* you were a tyrant. I needed that. It was part of being emotionally sick. I'm healthier now, but I don't feel strong enough to stand up to you."

"Jeanie, you're not going to need to do that."

She slammed the bat into his hip just on principle. She never broke her stride. "I believe you intend to be a partner in this marriage. You're sincere when you talk about your faith, but that means you're no longer the man I married. God has changed your heart and mine. He's created new people out of the ashes of the unhealthy marriage we had. Now you're like a stranger to me. A stranger who is living in my house. I hate that."

Jeanie stopped in the middle of the street. She saw a car coming two blocks away, the first that she'd seen in the middle of a work day at Cold Creek. It turned off before she needed to move to the side.

She crossed her arms to face Michael. "If you're not the tyrant I loved, then who are you? I might as well just pick a guy out at random and have *him* move in. I don't want you so close to me. I don't want any man, but most of all I don't want you." Jeanie stared at his handsome face. She'd fallen for him the first time he'd smiled at her. She'd been forbidden to date before she turned sixteen, but they'd started sneaking around together long before.

"I'm still the same man, Jeanie. My heart has changed. I'm a hard worker. I'm faithful. I've never cheated on you. I'm honest. Those are all part of me. Maybe, if we can get past that strange codependent thing we had where we found an almost sick pleasure in fighting and making up, we can rediscover the best of ourselves."

"I like being alone. I don't want to have a man or another child, ever. I blew my chance with Sally and you. I don't deserve another one."

Michael reached out and rested one hand on her arm. He didn't try to hang on or pull her close. Her bat was handy if he did. "Of course you deserve another chance. God forgives us. Everything about being a Christian is second chances."

Jeanie couldn't stand him touching her, so she turned and started moving again. Faster than ever.

Michael kept up. "You look fantastic. More beautiful than ever."

She swung the bat at his head and hoped it stung.

Michael smoothed his hair. "Why'd you do that?"

"Don't try to sweet-talk me. It makes my skin crawl." The truth was it made her skin shiver. Not at all like crawling.

How long had it been since a man had spoken flattering words to her? There'd been a few men in the last year, since she'd quit running and settled back in Cold Creek, who'd shown some interest. But she had mastered freezing men out. How galling to think she might have made herself vulnerable to Michael by her self-enforced loneliness. But what else could she have done? She was a married woman. She couldn't exactly date even if she'd wanted to—which she didn't.

She needed a bigger bat. Maybe oak. Better still—aluminum.

Main Street was coming up. The walk from the senior center was just under a mile. Jeanie didn't own a car, so she made the trek twice a day at least. The Golden Days Senior Center was just around the corner ahead. She felt like that was her goal, that she'd be safe when she arrived. But she was kidding herself. All of her trouble came right along with her. And it—*he*—had longer legs than she did. She had no more chance of escape than a cupcake at fat camp.

She met a couple of neighbors as she rounded the corner to Main Street. The post office was there, and it was more likely to have traffic than any other place in town.

She greeted her neighbors, and they had time to get her to agree to head the craft committee and the talent show for the

Memorial Day celebration. She promised again to come to the planning committee meeting tonight.

She felt Michael biting his tongue. Only the presence of witnesses kept her bat in check. But that wouldn't have saved him if he'd spoken. She didn't give a hoot if she embarrassed him.

They moved on toward the center, and Michael hustled a bit to grab the door and hold it for her. Nice manners. "You always were a gentleman, except when it came to treating me like a badly behaved child. Just that one little thing, endless emotional battering. Otherwise, Mr. Charm."

"Jeanie, I'm sorry."

Stepping into the center, she didn't reply. "Ten thirty. I'm right on time to put the final touches on dinner. So, you know how to peel potatoes?"

"Yes."

Jeanie sniffed. "I don't remember you ever helping with that at home. Did becoming a Christian make you start doing *women's work?*"

"Show me the potatoes and tell me how many to peel. You've got a lot of anger stored up, and I'm going to prove to you that I can take it. I deserve it, and you deserve a chance to vent."

Jeanie dumped a ten-pound bag of potatoes in the sink and snapped a peeler on the counter with a metallic click. She whacked him with the bat as he picked up the peeler.

"What's that for?"

"That's for giving me *permission* to be angry with the husband who deserted me and my child."

Michael started skinning the potatoes in silence.

She set the bat on the countertop so she could bake a couple of pans of brownies, but she kept it within grabbing distance.

seven

Michael was out of breath just keeping up with her.

They'd finished at the senior center, walked back to the nursing home—she'd worked a shift there—and visited her hospice patients who were residents of the manor. And the day wasn't over yet. They headed for the nursing home exit to—Michael presumed—walk another mile.

"Now you've got a town meeting? We've been up since 5:00 a.m., and I slept in my car last night." He jumped back, and the bat missed him.

Jeanie stopped and crossed her arms over Old Hickory. He knew that look. After one day he knew that look. "I'm sorry. It was instinct. Go ahead and let me have it."

He stepped closer but noticed she didn't bother to swing again. Was it possible her arm was tired? He was pretty sure that, even though it was latex and air, she'd left some bruises. The woman had a *lot* of suppressed anger.

"Well, I didn't sleep much at all. Having my husband show up and start screaming at me was pretty upsetting."

"I'm sorry." She didn't bother swinging. She was tired. Maybe now was a good time to try to make some headway in this mess of a marriage.

"I've studied the meaning of marriage. God's meaning. God called men to love their wives as Christ loved the church. Christ *died* for the church. He cried over it. He healed and performed miracles and pleaded and preached and walked all over the nation of Israel trying to spread His message of love. I'm going to do that for you, Jeanie. I promise before you and God. I've been convicted of the depth of my sin, and I only

39

want a chance to make it up to you. I owe you so much. I've hurt you so much. I've—"

"Enough!" Jeanie left the nursing home and set out for Main Street. Michael trailed along one leash short of heeling like a dog.

He had followed her like this all day. He'd tried to help in any way he could while Jeanie put in a four-hour shift. The nursing home administrator put him to work. They had a list a mile long ready for unsuspecting volunteers. He'd mowed and weeded flower beds and moved furniture. Then he'd folded laundry, dragging a basket of it with him while he visited with patients. Jeanie had directed him to two different rooms with people lying immobile in their beds, asleep or unconscious.

"Talk to them," she'd said. "They're my hospice patients."

Not eager to be turned into a line drive, he'd obeyed. At a loss, he'd told the patients about his bungled marriage. He hoped the sound of his own voice would give him some bright ideas. The folks he visited slept.

Now here they were off to a committee meeting. Michael sighed, but even that he did quietly. Maybe there was something to that bat. He was definitely beginning to think before he spoke.

People stood in line to hug his wife, and it chafed him. Michael waited patiently, but his jaw was tense until the warm greetings ended. He knew this reaction. He'd called it love when they were married, but it was jealousy—or more accurately, self-centeredness. He wanted Jeanie to stand slightly behind him while people made a fuss over him.

God, please make me a better man. Forgive me for my sins. Take away that old nature.

He noticed Carolyn Herne from the nursing home church service and saw the man who must be her husband, Mayor Bucky. His wife was a slim redhead, full of motion and energy.

Mayor Herne was grayer, rounder, and slower. But he had a great smile and a hearty manner that everyone responded to. The mayor took the center seat at a table at the front of the room. Two other men and one woman sat beside him.

The mayor rapped a gavel. They dispensed quickly with a roll call, minutes, and a treasurer's report. Then the mayor asked about new business and started talking. "All right, let's get the plans in motion for the Memorial Day celebration."

Jeanie and Michael sat at the back of the few short rows of chairs in the large auditorium. Michael quit listening. He prayed silently as he tried to look clearly at all the ins and outs of his selfishness. He was so focused on his prayers and asking for forgiveness and healing from what seemed like reactions imbedded on an instinctive level, terribly hard to overcome, he didn't notice the room had fallen silent for a while. He looked up.

Everyone stared at him.

"What?" He glanced at Jeanie for an explanation.

"I just told them you'd be involved with the Memorial Day celebration, too."

Michael only knew Jeanie was involved, and anything she did, he'd do. "That's right." He smiled at the gathered group of about twenty. "I want to help. You know Jeanie told me that the Shaw Ranch's buffalo are a pretty good tourist attraction. Maybe if you used—" Michael quit because Jeanie's fingernails had started digging into his forearm. If he kept talking, it might end up with him scarred for life. Some men got their wife's name tattooed on their arm. He'd have a slightly different permanent keepsake—claw marks.

"We thought this year we'd try to focus on the veterans more. We always do a ceremony at the city hall and end it at the cemetery, but we thought this time. . ."

Michael had felt a glimmer of excitement when he imagined the quiet little town bustling with tourists, tram rides out to the ranch, games and shows focusing on the former history of the area when buffalo roamed free, Wild West costumes, and maybe a small rodeo. Wild Bill Hickok was from South Dakota, wasn't he? Or Buffalo Bill Cody maybe? Deadwood. Mount Rushmore. Lots of possible ideas. And with Cold Creek flowing through town, wide enough for some water sports—at least canoeing or rafting or fishing tournaments—the town was full of possibilities. If they planned to play it safe instead of doing something exciting, he wasn't all that interested.

He mostly ignored the meeting, concentrating instead on praying for self-control and a miracle. He figured he needed both to win Jeanie back.

What little he caught was very routine. Standard Memorial Day fare. Blah, blah, blah, flags. Blah, blah, blah, trumpets. Blah, blah, blah, twenty-one-gun salute. Nothing much earthshaking there. Sure he'd help. Maybe they'd let him mow the grass at the cemetery or something. Jeanie, who kept raising her hand and saying, "I'll help," like some kind of jack-in-the-box, was probably already doing it, so he'd pitch in.

The meeting broke up, and the same round of hugs wore on his nerves.

Jeanie seemed to be quite the local celebrity. More likely the local doormat. Michael knew only too well she'd be good at that.

Pastor Bert had said she had a servant's heart. Well, the whole town had tapped into it. But not him. Oh no. The husband gets left out in the cold.

Everyone else left. He helped Jeanie fold up the chairs and return them to the rolling racks. When they were finished, she produced a key for the building.

How'd she get that?

They left through the back door of the aging Main Street structure that opened to the same alley containing Jeanie's staircase. She locked up, pocketed the key, and whacked him with the bat.

On about the fifth whack, when she showed no sign of stopping, he grabbed the stupid thing. "What did I do?"

She jerked it loose from his grip, but she stopped with the puffy beating. "I've known you a long time, Michael. I could read your mind. Well, what I do in this town is *my* choice. It's *my* life! You think I need to give up that life for you. I *won't*. Every time you grind your teeth or clench your jaw to keep from saying the bossy things you're thinking, I'm hitting you for that, too."

"That's not fair. I deserve some credit for controlling myself."

"You deserve *nothing*." With a guttural scream of frustration, she turned and marched toward her apartment, which meant she walked ten feet. "I can't believe I'm stuck with you tonight."

In all honesty, Michael couldn't believe it either.

"It won't last long. I've never seen you go a full day without losing your temper." She stomped up the old steps, making so much noise Michael was afraid the staircase might collapse. "I'll have you pitched out on your ear before the evening is over."

Michael jogged to catch up. "Let me take you out to supper. It's nine o'clock, I know, but you've barely eaten all day." He'd barely eaten either.

"Don't you mean *you've* barely eaten all day?"

"No, I'm just—I want to take care of you in some little way. Please, Jeanie? It's not about the food. It's about me trying to start, some little way, proving to you that I'm a changed man."

Jeanie snorted as she dug out her key for this ridiculous excuse for an apartment. If he rented a better place, she'd never agree to move into it with him, so he didn't say a word as he hurried inside, afraid she'd lock him out if she had the least chance.

"I told Mrs. Tippens you'd clean out her gutters tomorrow. She's living at the nursing home, but she still owns a house, and she worries about it."

"Mrs. Tippens? I remember her. She slept through the church service."

Jeanie's glare nearly caught his hair on fire. "She woke up once for a few minutes, and she frets. This will put her mind at ease. You clean gutters while I'm getting dinner at Golden Days."

"Okay, I'd be glad to."

Jeanie went into what might be laughingly described as the kitchen.

The whole main room of the apartment was about fifteen-by-fifteen feet. Three doors in the wall opposite where they'd come in were opened. One was Jeanie's bedroom, complete with a single bed. One was a tiny bathroom. The other seemed empty. He'd be sleeping there no doubt. He wondered if anyone in town sold inflatable mattresses.

The kitchen took up one corner. She opened a refrigerator circa 1950 and dragged out a loaf of bread and a couple of other things. "If you're hungry, I've got some sliced turkey." She set things on her countertop—which was two feet of cracked and curled black linoleum. She was so obviously making just one sandwich that Michael didn't hesitate. Good excuse to stand next to her anyway.

He built a nice turkey sandwich with mayo, dill pickles, cheese, and lettuce. He noticed she ate hers without mayo and with a meager serving of turkey. No wonder she was so thin. "After I'm done with Mrs. Tippens's gutters, I'll stop for groceries. I can help with the bills."

Jeanie turned on him. "You're not going to be here long enough to pay for anything."

Michael couldn't stop a smile when he heard the tone of her voice and saw the fire in her eyes.

"You think this is funny?"

"No, I think you're wonderful." He reached out, a little afraid he'd draw back a stump, but he couldn't resist resting his hand against her cheek. "I think I was a fool to try to mold you into some perfect, submissive wife, because I had no idea what perfect was. I love what you've become since you got away from me. I made it harder for you to get here, but you made it. I'm proud of you. Let's go sit on your couch and exchange our lists, like the pastor told us."

Jeanie's eyes wavered. She still loved him—he had to believe it. But she didn't trust him, and he had to respect that. She watched as he centered his sandwich on his plate, cut into two perfect triangles.

Jeanie had left hers whole, and it was far less tidy than Michael's. He knew, when they'd been together, he'd have said just a few mocking words about slapping a sandwich together. He'd have made sure she felt that little pinch of criticism. She hadn't been able to breathe to suit him during their entire marriage and most of their years of dating.

"You should have had a bat right from the first."

Jeanie looked at the bat she'd leaned against the refrigerator while she made her meal.

"I can't think of a single thing I love about you, Michael."

His stomach twisted as he internally rejected her words. "Well, I've got a lot I love about you, and I hope after we've been together for a while, you'll discover some things to love about me. I don't want it to be about before, because nothing we loved about each other was healthy. Let's go sit down."

He led the way, and when he sat down, he saw she'd brought along her trusty Louisville Slugger.

Michael had jotted a few things down. He pulled the list out of his jeans pocket.

eight

Jeanie saw that piece of paper and felt as if Michael were going to read her death certificate.

He'd always had a rare gift of charming her out of a bad mood—in the early days—when he'd tried. Later he'd just browbeaten her. She fought to keep cool, keep distant.

Michael sat on the couch, and Jeanie headed for the one overstuffed chair.

"Please sit beside me."

"Fine, let's hear this list." She sank onto her bristly, thread-bare couch, made sure there was three feet between them, and took a hefty bite out of her sandwich, barely resisting the urge to do something gross like chew with her mouth open or dribble crumbs on her lap. That'd make him crazy.

She braced herself to slap down every superficial thing he said. She expected to hear him claim to love all the things he'd tried to change.

"I love that you've become a woman of faith."

Well, rats. How was she supposed to slap that down? She took another bite to keep from telling him she was proud of his new faith, too.

"I love that you're caring for people in need. Your kindness was always the most alluring thing about you."

Jeanie rolled her eyes, wanting him to know she wasn't affected by his words—even though she was. She kept eating, and her sandwich was shrinking fast. What excuse was she supposed to have for silence once the food was gone?

"It's true, Jeanie. I took advantage of your sweetness and your low opinion of yourself. I grabbed you and started right in making sure you thought you were lucky to have me. You were funny and popular. You could have had any guy you wanted."

"I don't want a guy."

"I want you to know that I've been faithful to you these years we've been apart. I'm not going to claim it was because I'm so honorable. No man who abandons his family can kid himself about honor. But the truth is I threw myself into working after I left. I was so cocky." He clenched his fists and shook them. "So sure I could rule the world, be rich, show you, show *everyone* how great I was. I just focused only on that."

"Whatever." She did her best to act like it didn't matter— but it did. It mattered so terribly. She'd always pictured him leaving her for another woman. The thoughts had tormented her, deepened her sense of failure.

She set her empty plate aside and stared at her hands, folded in her lap like a good girl. The pastor had asked something of them, and Michael had delivered. Her husband-the-rat was sincere about his new faith. Three months ago he'd made a commitment to Christ. If she was too hard on him, could she possibly undermine a new baby Christian? She didn't want to mend their marriage. What could she do but be honest? God asked for nothing less.

"Michael, I'll tell you what I love about you." She met his eyes. His were a darker blue than hers. Right now they were locked on her, gazing, giving her a chance in a way he never had before.

"I'm a Christian. I became a Christian after I abandoned Sally. I ran off and left her, giving Buffy the papers she needed to begin adoption proceedings. When I left, I was as low as a person can sink. I hated myself, and I guess I'm not the suicidal type, because I never considered it, but I didn't feel like I deserved to live."

"Jeanie, I—"

"Stop." Jeanie held up her hand. She could see it cost him, but he quit talking. "I need to finish this."

Nodding, Michael subsided against the couch cushions, his lips clamped shut.

"I'm a believer. Jesus said plainly we're to love God and love our neighbors. Those are His greatest commandments. So I love you. I am happy for you that you've found Christ, and I can see the change in you. I can see you trying to be kind, and that's something you never wasted a second on before."

Michael rubbed his hand over his mouth, clearly trying to hold back words. His blatant regret weakened her resolve. If she gave him another chance, he really would try. She believed that. She also believed he'd fail.

"But as far as a romantic love, I just don't feel it. The only emotion you stir that isn't negative—and there are plenty of those—the only twinges of love I've had for you are sick. They seem like traces of that old dependence. I'm *afraid* of loving you. Honestly, Michael, loving you and mending our relationship might destroy me, and it might destroy you, too. Can you honestly say you're not afraid of slipping back into that awful excuse we had for a marriage?"

After so obviously wanting to interrupt her before, now he didn't speak. His shoulders slumped, and he set his own sandwich plate aside and reached out tentatively to take her hands. She almost pulled away, but his demeanor, so defeated and humble, was such a surprise that she hesitated and he had her. She decided not to dispute the touch—for now.

"I *am* afraid. I am. But I also believe God calls us to one marriage and the vows are for life. If we can't make our marriage work, then we both have to be alone forever. I don't want a life like that."

"I do."

Tightening his grip, he shook his head. "You only want to

be alone because I made it so bad for us. Maybe it's true that we can't be together. But I think we dishonor God by not at least trying."

Jeanie shook her head.

"We owe God that much." He threaded his fingers through hers. "We owe our faith that much—to try. Just walking away from each other isn't honoring our vows any more than divorcing would be. God asks more of us than that. We need to get to know each other. Really start over. Nothing that we had before is a foundation for a marriage, so we throw that out and get to know each other as if we were strangers. Because we are strangers. We're new people. New in Christ. Let's just start over." He eased his hands free and reached one out to shake. "It's the right thing to do, isn't it?"

"Why is 'the right thing to do' always what I *don't* want?"

"You're not the one who has the struggle ahead of you. Or if it is a struggle, it will be to keep me accountable. I'm the one who has to change. I'm the one who has anger and control issues knotted up inside. Give me a chance, please, Jeanie? Please?" His eyes pleaded. His words begged. His hand waited.

She couldn't tell him no. And hadn't that always been her fundamental problem? But this time, galling though it was, she felt the truth of it. They weren't honoring their marriage vows by living separately and alone for the rest of their lives.

Heart sinking, tears threatening, she reached out. Their hands met and held. "All right. I'll try." Tears spilled over as they shook.

He pulled her forward and held her, hugging her. She didn't realize how long it had been since someone had really held her. Not a brief hello hug, but real contact. The loneliness of her life made her cling to him—in joy for the human touch and in despair because she sensed she'd just taken her first step toward self-destruction.

nine

Michael took his cue from Jeanie and began simply to say yes when something was asked of him.

It took less than a week before he'd gained a reputation as someone who'd lend a hand, and besides what he did for free, he made a few dollars. He was the Cold Creek handyman—a big change from a shark hustling building contracts.

He mowed lawns, did minor household repairs, fixed leaky faucets. He charged next to nothing and often didn't ask for money at all.

It was a way to make a living. The business and marketing strategy of his corporation consisted of hand-printed signs taped up at the senior center, grocery store, bank, and mini-mart.

He joined the volunteer fire department, chipped in on all the Memorial Day committees that were shorthanded, and agreed to help with the Monday morning church service at the nursing home.

He did as much with Jeanie as he could, but when their lives pulled them in separate directions, he went where he was needed, because he sensed Jeanie respected his willingness to serve others and he wanted her respect.

He returned his rented car to Rapid City and came home with a small pickup, careful not to buy anything too flashy, even though he could well afford it.

They'd been together five days when he came home one evening and announced fearfully, "Jeanie, I bought a house."

"What?"

He lifted both hands as if he were warding off a pit bull. "Listen, I didn't do it to control you or to judge where you live. I was repairing a drainpipe on Myra Dean's house, and her son showed up. He lives out of town, and we got to talking. He told me he really needed to get some money out of the house."

"You bought Myra's house?"

Michael had run himself ragged serving coffee at her funeral.

"Her family has a lot of bills to pay for the nursing home and the funeral, and they had no prospects. I promise I paid an honest price." A steal is what it was. If that huge old house had been sitting in Chicago somewhere, it would have cost a half million dollars. He'd bought it for fifty thousand, and Lance had practically wept with gratitude.

"It's a white elephant. It's practically falling down. It's been sitting empty for three years since Myra moved into the nursing home."

Michael shook his head. "It's been neglected, but it's got great bones, a solid foundation. And I love that American foursquare architecture. I'll enjoy refurbishing it. I had to do it for Myra's son, didn't I?"

Jeanie shook her head. "Yes, you're right." She whacked him with the bat. "But you should have talked to me first."

"It was a spur of the moment thing. I'm sorry."

"I'm busy. I'm not helping you pack and move."

"I'll close on it tomorrow and move everything by the weekend. You'll live with me in it, won't you? If not, we'll just stay here."

Jeanie knew Myra, and she knew the years in the nursing home had cost her family a lot. The Dean family did need the cash. "Yes, I'll live there."

"Thanks. I promise you won't have to lift a finger."

Jeanie rolled her eyes at him and turned to the kitchen to pull a pizza out of the oven. Frozen.

Michael felt lucky that she hadn't bought a personal pan

size. She was cooking dinner for both of them. He was tempted to jump up and down and yell, but he was afraid the bat would come out.

Working on so many aspects of the Memorial Day celebration got him involved. Maybe too involved. The weekend events bothered him for their complete lack of flare, and he convinced the town fathers to let him put a couple of ads in the Rapid City paper, at his expense, to lure in tourists interested in the buffalo. He enlisted a couple of area seniors to be available to drive a minivan out to the herd if anyone showed up wanting to pay for the privilege.

And he met his daughter.

"She's huge." Michael caught Jeanie's hand, his eyes riveted on Sally. He took a step toward the little blond beauty, and someone blocked his path. He was so diverted by Sally he ran headlong into Buffy—his sister-in-law with the temperament of a buffalo.

"I heard you'd shown up in town." Buffy jammed her fists onto her hips and looked as if she'd tear into him with the least provocation. Michael sincerely hoped no one gave *her* a bat.

Buffy was two years younger than Jeanie, but they'd been in the same grade because of Buffy's genius IQ. While Jeanie played, Buffy studied. While Jeanie flirted, Buffy worked nights and weekends at a nearby wildlife park just outside Chicago. Buffy was lean and had dark, straight hair. He remembered she'd always worn it in a braid, but today it hung in loose, gentle curls. Then, as now, she'd ignored makeup. She'd been very solemn and quiet. The complete opposite of his blond, blue-eyed, flirty, flashy Jeanie.

She was six years younger than Michael, and back in high school, even from that disadvantaged level, she'd told him to his face he was scum for hanging around a girl as young as her sister. At the time he'd hated the little brat. Plain, no flare, no humor, no personality. But even then he'd recognized her as a better person than either Jeanie or him. Her words had echoed in his head like a sleeping conscience. And that only made him hate her more.

Maybe it was because he'd finally grown up, but he noticed immediately that she'd become a beautiful woman. Grouchy but beautiful.

"This is that no-account coyote who abandoned Sally?" A gruff voice pulled Michael's eyes up and up until they met Wyatt Shaw's. He stood behind Buffy. Jeanie had said Buffy's new husband was a rancher, but Michael would have known it at a glance. The weathered skin, dark hair hanging a bit long below a gray Stetson, and an attitude as cold as a South Dakota winter. Wyatt held his little girl, Audra, in his huge, work-scarred hands. Patting the toddler's back while the baby giggled until her dark curls bounced muted Wyatt's arctic demeanor.

Michael knew he deserved this scorn, and he was determined to stand here and take it like a man.

"This is him." Buffy turned her eyes on Jeanie, and Michael braced himself to protect his wife.

"Aunt Jeanie!" A small blond tornado hit Jeanie in the legs. Michael saw Sally up close at last.

Aunt Jeanie. The words registered and cut like a knife.

Then two more balls of energy came onto the scene. Wyatt had twin sons.

Michael couldn't take his eyes off of Sally, the image of Jeanie.

Then Buffy caught his arm.

Reluctantly, he turned.

"We need to talk. You've got"—Buffy glanced at Sally, who was talking nonstop to Jeanie, along with the twins who were as identical as mirror images—"papers we need signed."

Michael clenched his jaw. Now wasn't the time or place to

tell Buffy that he intended to get back together with Jeanie and reclaim his daughter. He nodded. "We do need to talk."

"After church. We can send the kids to a friend's house for lunch and have this out."

Michael wasn't quite ready to have anything out. He suspected that, as things stood, for him to start a fight over Sally might be the last straw with Jeanie. She'd kick him out and there'd be no further chance of reconciliation. But he had until the end of summer to protest the termination of his parental rights. He didn't need to tell anyone anything right now. He'd let things bump along as they were until he'd renewed his marriage.

"Fine, after church." He had one hour to figure out just what he was going to say. For now, he decided to change the subject to the one thing that might possibly distract his cranky sister-in-law. "Has the mayor contacted you about the buffalo excursions for Memorial Day?"

Buffy scowled. "We agreed to move a small group to the holding pens closer to town so the ride won't be so long and the buffalo will be close to the road."

"Good. That's settled then. You draw some tourists, right?"

Buffy nodded. "We do."

"Do you have any pamphlets we could spread around to advertise the buffalo?"

"We've got something." Wyatt caught Buffy's arm and added, "Come on, kids. The parson's getting read to start."

The twins and Sally whined and said a lot of good-byes to Jeanie without so much as looking Michael's way. His own daughter had walked right past him and had no idea who he was. It was like taking a knife to the heart. And it was a knife thrust by his own hand. His choices, his selfishness had led him to this pain.

He felt a hand on his elbow and looked up. Jeanie's sympathy was plain to see. She knew how he felt. Their eyes held.

What was it she'd said? "God has forgiven me for that, but I'll never forgive myself." The difference was he'd brought her to the point where she'd abandoned Sally. Whatever forgiveness she needed, he needed a hundred times more.

She tugged on his arm and led him into a pew near the back of the hundred-year-old church. Then she went up front to the piano and accompanied the organist.

Michael felt abandoned though he was fiercely proud of how well Jeanie played.

The Shaws were sitting about five rows ahead. Michael could watch Sally whisper to her father—Wyatt Shaw, not Michael—with adoring eyes. That was what he'd thrown away.

His eyes burned, but he refused to let the tears fall. Instead, they stayed inside, cutting his heart like acid rain.

ten

Michael deserved whatever he got.

Even so, Jeanie felt an almost compulsive need to protect Michael from Buffy, which was stupid, but she couldn't help herself. She prayed for this "talk" as she played the hymns.

Buffy had such a decent heart, she couldn't be truly cruel to anyone. She'd allowed Jeanie back into the family as an aunt. And they were closer now than they'd ever been, real friends. They worshipped together because Jeanie had returned to Cold Creek and started attending here about a year after she'd abandoned Sally.

Buffy had included Jeanie in get-togethers with her friend, Emily Hanson, another woman about their age, and Emily had become an even better friend than Buffy.

But Buffy had no use for Michael. Never had.

When church broke up, Jeanie left her place at the piano, fighting the urge to grab Michael and run.

But why? Let Buffy have at him. Wanting to protect her jerk of a husband was just a leftover reflex from long ago.

Jeanie emerged from church, aware Michael had a firm hold on her arm. Normally she'd have shaken him off. No bat at church, but if she would have had it, she would have whacked him, except she felt sorry for the big goon.

Jeanie saw Buffy waving good-bye to the kids as they drove away with Emily and her husband, Jake. Emily was far along in a pregnancy, but she didn't hesitate for a second to let the three rambunctious Shaw kids into her car.

Buffy turned to Michael, Audra in her arms. Wyatt relieved her of the baby, as if to get the child to shelter.

Michael headed straight for Buffy. No running and hiding for Michael Davidson, he seemed determined to take his tongue-lashing like a man. Though his steps were firm, his voice was gentle. "Buffy, before we start, I want you to know I've become a Christian since I left Jeanie and Sally. I'm back to make things right." Michael settled himself, his feet slightly spread, as if he expected Buffy to start swinging and he was going to take the whole thing standing.

"I want those papers signed before one more day goes by. You've—"

"I'm glad you're all together." Bucky Herne approached the group, not aware he'd stepped into a kill zone. He directed his words to Wyatt. "I've got to get things squared away about the buffalo for Memorial Day."

Buffy's eyes narrowed at the mayor. Jeanie could read Buffy's mind. She took care of the buffalo herd. For that matter, this whole thing was Michael's idea, and Jeanie volunteered to do almost all the work. And yet the mayor talked to Wyatt. Wyatt's family had been here five generations. Roots bought respect in South Dakota.

Michael turned to the mayor and cocked his head and focused. How well Jeanie remembered that focus. The man could make you feel like the center of the universe. That's how he'd made her feel at first. Later she'd been more like a bug under a microscope.

"Bucky, I've written up some detailed notes about Memorial Day. The Shaws are willing to bring about twenty head of buffalo to the holding pens near town."

Jeanie saw Bucky switch his attention from Wyatt, who wasn't interested at any rate, to Michael. The older man practically preened under Michael's respectful forcefulness.

"And about rides out there—," the mayor said.

"At first we planned on having a few Cold Creek residents lend their minivans. But I've gotten such a good response from the ads—it included a phone number to book the bus tour in advance—that I rented a bus from Rapid City. It's comfortable and seats about forty people. This will be at my expense, because I'm the one proposing it, and I don't want the city to take any financial risks. I'll make sure any profits go into the city coffers, too. And I've already arranged some publicity. *The Rapid City Journal* and the *Hot Springs Star* will run a story, and two of the local television stations have asked for interviews. Area radio stations have. . ."

Michael just took off talking and left them all in his dust. Jeanie had heard about the rented buses, but TV and the biggest newspaper in the area? She'd never heard a peep. How like Michael to just start handling things.

The mayor looked dazed. Wyatt looked intrigued as he bounced his little girl in his arms. Buffy looked irritated. She hadn't forgotten those adoption papers. And then the car with her—Jeanie flinched—*Buffy's* three kids came driving back into the church parking lot at top speed.

The three Shaw children jumped out of the car. Jake swung his door open with a wild expression on his face. "Hey, I'm sorry about this, but Emily's water just broke. We need to get to the hospital. We can't take the kids after all."

"That's fine." Wyatt waved. "You want us to take Stephie?"

"Nope, she wants to go along. Thanks, though." He swung the door shut and tore off.

Their little group grew, with the children adding to the chaos.

Two more parishioners and the pastor came up, and the Memorial Day committee began an impromptu meeting.

Buffy gave Michael a look that would have left a lesser man writhing in pain on the ground. Michael was too busy holding court to notice.

Jeanie went to Buffy's side. "We'll get it signed. Michael is determined to fix our marriage, and he has convinced me to at least try. I've been—" Jeanie realized Michael was inches away, and the man could multitask like nobody's business. He'd hear this, plus the children were swarming around everyone.

Jeanie pulled Buffy aside.

"I'll talk to him. He's only got about three months left until the deadline, so even if he does nothing, it'll be over soon." Tears suddenly cut across Jeanie's eyes, and she dashed a hand across them quickly, glad she didn't wear mascara anymore.

Buffy's hand rested on Jeanie's arm. "You know this is for the best."

Jeanie nodded. "It is. Even if Michael and I fix things, she"—Jeanie's gaze darted toward Sally—"is your daughter. We won't do anything to harm her."

Buffy looked skeptical. "Your husband has a knack for twisting the world to suit himself. I won't rest easy until he's signed those papers."

Jeanie had a moment of doubt. Michael hadn't said loud and clear that Sally's adoption was all right with him. At first he'd been furious. Then, when he found out Sally was in good hands, he'd accepted it. Or had he? Jeanie hadn't trusted Michael for a long time.

"We don't have a motel or any overnight accommodations." Mayor Herne tugged on his tie to loosen the knot, then pulled it all the way off, wrapped it around his hand, and slipped the tie in his suit coat pocket. The day was warm for early May.

"Nothing for overnight?" Michael rubbed his chin with one thumb. "Memorial Day is a three-day weekend. To really make some money with tourism, we need somewhere for folks to stay."

"Do you have the papers, Jeanie?" Buffy drew Jeanie back to the most important matter at hand. "I've got copies if you need them."

"Mike has the ones he's supposed to sign. And I promise I'll talk to him. This isn't the time or place."

"I'm starving, Dad." Cody or Colt, Jeanie could never tell them apart, tugged on Wyatt's arm.

"So if we could get a few people to maybe open up their homes, like a bed and breakfast, just for the weekend—"

"Well, I don't know about that." The mayor shrugged off his suit coat. "I mean, strangers in your house? Not too many folks will want that."

"Jeanie and I just bought a house. We've moved in, and we've only got a few pieces of furniture. But it's a neat old place. We could furnish a few more bedrooms, even move back to her apartment for the weekend."

"We've got to go, Buff. The kids are starving." Wyatt came over, Audra in one arm, both twins nagging that they were starving.

Buffy shook her head in defeat. "Okay." She glared at Michael, who glanced up and caught the look. The mayor was talking to Pastor Bert.

"We'll talk later, Buffy. I promise." Michael jerked his head at Sally as if that was what prevented him from saying more.

Buffy's eyes narrowed. It wasn't lost on Jeanie, nor Buffy, that Michael could easily promise to sign Buffy's papers without Sally understanding.

"I promise right back." Buffy made it a threat as she laid her hand on Sally's shoulder. "Let's go, honey. Mommy's got dinner in the oven, and the boys are starving."

"I've been thinking I might put up some A-frame buildings. Something really simple. A row of ten maybe. I could build them myself. There's a nice spot along Cold Creek right on the edge of town. I think it's part of the city's right-of-way, so the town council would have to approve it or sell it to me or whatever. And we could rent them out. I might be able to get a couple up by Memorial Day."

Jeanie stood watching Sally be driven away in a cloud of dust.

Watching Michael wheel and deal.

Watching her life slip completely out of her control.

And the worst part of Michael being back was Jeanie didn't *want* to be in control. She wanted to take orders and be obedient. It was easy and wrong. God didn't want her to give the reins of her life over to anyone but Him.

She stared at the group of movers and shakers, the biggest one of all in the very center of the action. Yes, the Peaceful Mountain Church was in the country. Yes, it was a five-mile walk home up and down a mountain pass and along a narrow country highway. Yes, she'd ridden here in Michael's new pickup. None of that mattered.

She needed to get out of here. He'd come for her before she got home. A new home she'd been moved into with precious little consultation. He'd pick her up whenever he came. It would be all too soon.

She wondered if Pastor Bert would allow her to bring her bat to church.

eleven

The Memorial Day celebration got way out of hand for a normal human being.

Jeanie had never accused Michael of being normal.

Shaking her head, she watched her husband plot and plan with the city fathers about making it a real tourist event.

The media was involved.

Cold Creek was buzzing.

Michael was in his element. He bought what looked to everyone else in the world like wasteland along the steep banks of Cold Creek. Michael's sharp eyes saw a gold mine. He was single-handedly building a motel. A row of simple, rustic A-frames with roofs slanting all the way to the ground. He did the planning, the buying, the bulldozing, the sawing, and the nailing himself.

Except Jeanie knew him too well. He *didn't* do it himself. He just *started* it alone. Before the end of the first day, everyone in town was helping.

Jeanie remembered the story "Stone Soup." Michael started out with a stone and a dream, and everyone else threw in.

Two retired plumbers offered to help. The proud owner of a bulldozer had been bulldozed into volunteering his time and machine. The women were sewing curtains, the businesses were donating material, and the excitement only grew as Michael announced, one by one, that the little cabins were rented out. . .before they were built.

"You want me to what?" Jeanie had taken two weeks off from the nursing home and her other part-time jobs to help with the project. Some of the other nurse's aides put in longer hours to cover for her.

"Open a restaurant. The old gas station would make a great café and gift shop. I bought it this morning for just a few hundred dollars."

The decrepit stone building so close at hand had been abandoned for years. But as Michael did that magical thing with words and the force of his will, Jeanie completely saw his vision.

"We could clean it out in a few days. We can't bring it up to specs for a restaurant in time, but we could have food catered in. I've already mentioned it to Glynna Harder. You know what a great cook she is. We could offer sandwiches and soup and a few other things. All we need is a clean building and tables. I've already asked around town and found a few people who have tables in their garages and basements that they'd like to get rid of. And the used junk store has several they'll sell us cheap."

Jeanie went to work and found herself with a lot of help. The women of Cold Creek had been itching to get more involved, and the heavy work of the construction was beyond most of them.

The week ticked away, and Jeanie found herself too busy during the day and too tired at night to spend any time on her marriage or to pin Michael down about Sally's adoption papers. She didn't even have the energy to bat him.

They dragged home hours after dark and were up before the sun. Michael had ordered two sets of bedroom furniture and had it delivered. Jeanie slept in one corner of the huge upstairs, and Michael slept three rooms down and across the hall. He hadn't even tried to weasel his way into Jeanie's room.

He'd turned one downstairs room into an office with phone lines, a computer, Internet access, and a desk and filing cabinet. Another phone call. The man had no time to browse;

he just phoned, ordered top of the line, and had it delivered and installed.

Jeanie still worked at Golden Days Senior Center through the morning, and Pastor Bert came into the center early, as he had that first day, and met with them weekly. A lot of Jeanie's volunteer work was suspended because so many of the people were working with Michael.

As Memorial Day crept closer, a party atmosphere grew in town until the community of Cold Creek became as close as family.

Michael had set out to build ten cabins, hoping to have three or four done in two weeks. He finished all ten. They were livable, and they'd all been rented. Michael had plans for ten more by the Fourth of July.

The gas station had become Jeanie's Café and was clean and shining inside. The mismatched tables and chairs were charming. The dinnerware was foraged from several auctions and junk stores in the area, and it lent the place a homey atmosphere. There was a lot more she could do with it, but it was useable for this one weekend.

When they finished for the night on the Thursday before the big weekend, Michael slung his arm around Jeanie, and they walked home, exhausted as usual. When they pushed their way through the sticking door of their new house, Michael smiled at her. "I've got all those buildings up, and I haven't done a thing to make this house more livable. 'The cobbler's children have no shoes.' Isn't that the saying?"

Jeanie smiled back. "It's okay. I love the work we're doing."

"I'm so proud of all you've accomplished with that gas station." Michael hugged her neck closer as he turned to close the door behind them. He dragged her just a bit, and she giggled and jabbed him in the ribs.

Flinching and laughing, he turned to her. "I didn't dare to hope it would look that good this fast."

"It's wonderful, isn't it? And I've got a lot of women lined up to bring in some crafts for the weekend. And there are more who want to be involved by Independence Day. And we've got fresh jelly, and there's a man bringing in honey to sell. It's your energy that's made it all happened, Mike."

"Maybe I started it, but it's a team effort. What's been accomplished is about everyone pulling together."

Jeanie wrapped her arms around his middle, since he wasn't letting go of her anyway. "I'm glad you came. I've loved having you back. I love—" Jeanie found herself caught by Michael's warm eyes.

Michael's smile faded as they stood. "We're together aren't we? Together in this marriage for the first time and forever."

"Yes." Jeanie's answer was a whisper.

Pulling back, Michael asked, "Were you going to say it?"

Jeanie knew what he meant. She still had doubts. Not doubts their marriage would work—she believed that was possible now—but doubts that they were ready for what she saw, right now, in Michael's eyes. But he was wonderful, and his arms felt so good.

"I was going to say, I love you." Jeanie hugged him. "And in the middle of all this, I remembered why I fell in love with you to begin with. I remembered the good things."

"Were there any good things?"

Jeanie sobered. "I fell so hard for you so fast. I was so proud of you. You're a leader, but you're generous, too. The way you've helped this town is just your nature. You have great vision and enthusiasm. I saw that in you when you were nineteen years old, and it's still there. . .that charm, the work ethic, the joy for life."

Brow furrowed, Michael said, "Our life together wasn't joyful. I don't want you to forget that. I'm almost afraid to let you love me. I want it so desperately." He hugged her again, lifting her to her toes. Then he set her down. "But I'm afraid I'll forget what a jerk I can be, and it'll happen all over again."

"I won't let you forget."

"Good girl." Michael lowered his head. "I love you, Jeanie. And this time I really know what that means."

Jeanie set aside her doubts and stretched up to meet her husband's lips.

Moments passed, long wonderful moments.

Then, his heart in his eyes, Michael asked, "We're together again, aren't we?" He ran one finger down her cheek, outlining her lips, tracing her jaw.

"Yes." Jeanie turned her head and kissed his palm, but a niggling of fear wouldn't let her give in to what Michael was obviously asking. "Yes, we're really together. And this time it's forever. But I don't think we're ready—at least I'm not."

Jeanie could see Michael fight the urge to push his wants on her, pressure her into accepting their marriage in all its fullness. But he won that fight. "I'll wait as long as you need. Hearing you say you love me is enough for now. It's what I've been praying for."

Relieved, Jeanie kissed him again.

Then they separated for their private rooms.

❧

Michael sang while he worked the next day.

Only finishing touches to ten proud little triangles of unfinished wood along the creek. Inside, each cabin was one main room with bare stud walls, no insulation or dry wall, twenty-four by twenty-four feet square at the base, rising to a peaked roof. A cement floor covered with cheap linoleum. A tiny bathroom—each cabin's only amenity besides a bed and electric lights—was partitioned out of each main room.

He'd rented these out so fast he knew he could build fifty more and keep them full. Line the whole creek bank on both sides. Maybe build a swinging footbridge and create some hiking trails. It was a beautiful, rustic spot. He had plans to polish the cabins up a bit, make them tight for winter and add heating and a tiny kitchen area. Rent them to tourists in the summer, ice fishermen in the winter, and hunters in the spring and fall. The smell of fresh wood and the outdoors was like the finest perfume. He was sure the customers would love them.

And speaking of love. . .

He pressed his hand flat to massage his heart. He'd glanced behind him a hundred times all through the morning, waiting for Jeanie to finish at the senior center and come to him. He could barely breathe when he thought of how madly in love he was.

God, forgive me for that awful excuse for love we shared before. Thank You, thank You, thank You for blessing me with my wife back. I didn't deserve it.

His eyes welled with tears as he remembered and cherished the new beginning.

God, thank You, thank You, thank You.

He couldn't say it enough times. He couldn't say it humbly enough. He couldn't ever begin to be worthy of this blessing.

He felt her and turned. Of course he'd turned around a hundred times before, thinking that he'd felt her those times, too.

She walked toward him, her hair pulled back in its no-nonsense ponytail, dressed in the jeans and T-shirt she wore to work. He dropped the broom he'd been using to sweep wood chips away from the front doors of his cabins and ran toward her. She was already nearly jogging, but when he ran, she raced to meet him.

Michael swept her into his arms in front of the refurbished gas station. When the kiss ended, Michael swung her in a circle. "I've been watching for you all morning."

They were alone. The rest of the town was sprucing up their homes and streets to welcome the holiday crowds.

Jeanie laughed. "I set a new record cleaning up after dinner."

Michael set her feet back on the ground, and they just held each other. Michael cherished every breath, every moment, every touch.

Thank You, God. Thank You. Thank You.

"Are we going to stand here holding each other all day?" Jeanie asked.

"How about until we die of old age?" Michael kissed the top of her head, her temple, her eyes.

"I want to hold on to you for that long, Michael."

He kissed her soundly. "Good. Then we're in total agreement." He squeezed until her feet lifted off the ground and she squeaked. He set her down, laughing. "Now, what have we got left to do before the first renter arrives?"

They worked companionably together for several hours, having fun making the cabins perfect.

Then their first guest arrived. The day got hectic as Jeanie took the vacationers into the café to register and Michael helped with the luggage.

Glynna arrived with her neat foil containers of hot savory roast beef and side dishes. The guests ate as fast as Glynna and Jeanie spooned the food, and the rustic cash register they had found abandoned in the building rang up sale after sale.

It was early evening by the time there was a letup. The Buffalo Bus was ready, and rides had been scheduled for the morning. The cabins were full, Jeanie's café-in-training was cleaned and set up for breakfast, and Jeanie and Michael made their way home, tired but overjoyed with the success of the day.

They were a couple, Michael knew, in a way they'd never been before. Married in their hearts and souls and minds.

Married in the way God intended.

ം

Jeanie ran nonstop the whole weekend.

The activity was laced with joy as she watched Michael

shine. He had a knack for bringing everyone along with him when he was enthusiastic.

Glynna's food sold out every meal. The Buffalo Bus was a huge hit, with people driving in for the day to ride it along with the people staying in the cabins.

The senior citizens had a fund-raising dinner Saturday at noon that had Jeanie running back and forth between that building and her café. But with all the extra hands helping in both places, she kept up and had fun.

On Sunday they had a community worship service in the park, and Monday morning featured the traditional Memorial Day program at the city auditorium. When the veterans marched in with the American flag, an army band Michael had arranged struck up *The Star-Spangled Banner*. Pride nearly vibrated the building.

By the time everyone checked out of the cabins on Monday and the Buffalo Bus had made its last run, Jeanie was ready to collapse; but it was a good kind of exhaustion.

Michael helped her lock up the café. "You're a fantastic cook, Jeanie. Glynna did a great job, but I'd love some of your homemade bread on the menu. Do you think Glynna would maybe partner with you when we get the building up to specs? You'll need waitresses and at least one more cook. By Independence Day I'd like to. . ."

Jeanie listened with tired amusement as they walked through the darkened streets, trees sighing overhead in the cool May breeze. Nightingales setting their walk to music. The homes were mostly darkened, though an occasional window glowed with light.

Michael drew energy from people and plans, and she remembered, years ago, that she'd been a social butterfly, too.

"You keep planning and arranging, but tomorrow I go back to my normal life. I've got to work morning and afternoon. They let me off at the nursing home for the last two weeks, and I took time off from my other jobs, too. But people have been taking extra shifts to fill in."

Michael stopped so suddenly that Jeanie stumbled. He turned. "What other jobs?"

"I help out at the library on Thursday nights and at the mini-mart two Saturdays a month."

"You haven't done that since I've been back, not even those first two weeks."

"You knew I went to the library on Thursdays."

"That was a job? I thought you were volunteering."

"No, I get paid. And I only work two Saturdays a month at the mini-mart, and you came on an off week. Then I asked for a break because of all this activity, but—"

Michael pulled her so tight against him that she couldn't finish making her point. But she suspected he got the gist.

"What do you think about quitting the extra jobs? Maybe the senior center, too? I've got five of the cabins rented out for next week. Not just a couple of weekend nights—the whole week. We're going to want to keep Jeanie's Café open. It's not like the little bit of money you bring in from these part-time jobs is important. I can support us."

Jeanie worried her bottom lip as she considered it. "I like the work I do. There's a real need, Michael."

"I agree. You can't quit unless there's someone to fill the void." He rested his hands on her shoulders. "You've done so much for this town."

Jeanie shook her head with a smile. "You've done more in, what—a month?—than I did in a year."

"But what you did, giving to people, even if it was just one at a time, like with your hospice work, was the real thing. True Christian service. Pastor Bert was dead right about that." Michael rested one hand on her chest. "That's your gift. This generous heart. And I'm benefiting from it because only someone as generous as you would have forgiven me."

Michael suddenly wrapped one arm around her shoulder and practically dragged her toward their shabby old house. "Let's go home."

Jeanie raced along with him. She didn't want to give up her jobs. The truth was she got so much more than she ever gave in her work. If she helped others, that was wonderful, but those people—the elderly, the library patrons, the children in 4-H and Girl Scouts—made her feel worthwhile. She'd known since she started this whirlwind of volunteering that it was rooted in her own sense of failure and selfishness.

As if she could be good enough, generous enough, self-sacrificing enough to deserve God's love. But she knew in her heart that she couldn't earn salvation. It was a free gift, and her nearly frantic efforts to be worthy were misguided. It was time she let go of her past failure and forgave herself.

So, if Michael wanted her to quit, she should.

She would quit in an orderly way so no one was left in need, but she *would* quit and cut back on her volunteer work. She'd devote herself to her marriage and Michael's vision for Cold Creek and try, finally, to forgive herself.

It was scriptural that she'd let Michael be the head of the house. He wanted her to quit. She'd quit.

Turning to Michael as they entered the house, she opened her mouth to tell him all of this. They were new people in Christ. Their marriage was new, and it was based on complete honesty. This was something she needed to share and work through with her husband.

Before she could speak, his lips met hers, and she knew without a doubt that Michael wasn't in the mood to have a heart-to-heart talk. As she wrapped her arms around him, she decided it could wait.

twelve

"I want to give notice that I'm quitting." Jeanie smiled at Tim Russo, the owner of the mini-mart.

She knew she'd really helped by working two Saturdays a month. The store was family-owned, and the long hours and hectic schedule of the place was a strain. Their profit margin was slim, and they couldn't pay much. Her help had given the family their only day off twice a month.

The money wasn't good enough to tempt many people, and her boss looked at her in dismay. "I can't say I'm surprised. We really appreciate your help this last year. It's made a world of difference in our family to have that free time." Tim smiled, but he looked worried. "I feel like my kids have gotten to know me again." He squared his shoulders. "But this year, well, they've gotten older. They've started working with me on the Saturdays you don't come in. We'll get by."

"I can keep working until you find someone to take my shift." Her heart sinking, Jeanie nearly backed down and agreed to stay on, but she'd made her decision. She hadn't told Michael yet. She'd decided to surprise him instead.

"No need. We'll be fine." Tim rested one burly hand on her shoulder. "We really appreciate your help. We'll try, but we won't be able to replace you. No, your husband's back, and you two need time together. I understand that better than anybody. Consider yourself fired." He shooed her good-naturedly toward the door.

Jeanie felt bad about it, but she thanked him and left for the library.

There the mini-mart scene was repeated. The librarian,

Julia Leesmith, was a retired schoolteacher, and the library was open only part-time. She insisted she didn't mind going back to her Thursday night schedule, although she'd have to give up a ladies' group that met once a month.

The nursing home was harder. She knew they were short-handed to begin with, employing lots of high schoolers who were notorious for needing time off for school events. The administrator took her up on her offer to stay until they found a replacement. She'd still be there for her hospice work and the Monday church service, but she'd grown fond of the residents of Cold Creek Manor as well as her coworkers and felt as if she was abandoning friends in need.

By evening Jeanie was near tears. Determined not to dump her emotional distress on Michael when he was still flying from the triumph of the holiday weekend, she had dinner ready by the time he got home. She remembered he'd insisted on that before.

Sliding a plate of meatloaf and mashed potatoes in front of him—it had been his favorite before, and Jeanie had carefully listened to his mother and learned to make it perfectly—she announced, "I've started simplifying my life."

Michael looked up from his plate. "What do you mean?"

Jeanie smiled and tried to make it look sincere even though her heart was breaking. "I told the mini-mart, the library, and the nursing home that I quit. The nursing home is the only place that asked me to stay on until they can find a replacement. So I'll be down to one job soon."

"Did they say how long it will take to find a replacement?" Michael tapped the white stoneware plate with his fork.

Jeanie had found the dishes and silverware used for a few dollars. Except for the bedrooms, their house was furnished out of junk stores with her meager apartment furniture. She was surprised Michael put up with it. But he'd been busy.

"They could string you along. You probably should have

just given them two weeks' notice."

Jeanie gave him a saucy smile that she'd never dared give him in their earlier years. "Well, of course they're going to string me along. They're very sorry to lose me."

Michael smiled, but it didn't reach his eyes.

She hurried to reassure him. "The administrator is a good man. He'll respect my request. But the LPN program is hinged on me putting in some hours. I've been carpooling to a community college to take classes once a week. We're on break now, but classes start again in the fall, and my work counts toward course credits. If I quit completely, I'll lose the credit I've built up. I'd like to finish that. Have my license."

Michael's eyebrows lowered. "You don't need the license. You're not going to go back to that kind of work."

"I—I might someday."

"Why would you? I'm going to take care of you now."

Jeanie didn't respond. To say she wanted to be able to take care of herself seemed like she didn't trust him. "It would just give me a great feeling of accomplishment to finish what I started."

"We'll have to see if you've got time. You can try to get the hours in." Scooping meatloaf into his mouth, Michael chewed and swallowed. "This is Mom's recipe, isn't it?"

Jeanie's heart perked a bit. He'd noticed. "Yes, it was always your favorite."

"It's delicious, but it's no wonder Dad died of a heart attack, adding cheese and this sweet sauce to it. Fat and calories. Did you buy lean hamburger?"

"The local store doesn't have much of a selection." Jeanie began revamping the recipe.

"What about the senior center? When will you tell them you're quitting?"

She hadn't until this moment let herself think about Golden Days. She'd miss them so much. Tears burned as she remembered how those folks had opened their hearts to her when she arrived in Cold Creek, a new Christian. Her new baby faith had grown under their kindness. No, she didn't have a servant's heart at all, no matter what others said. Every time she helped someone, she received more than she gave.

Grateful that Michael was fixated on the meal, she fought back the tears and quickly swiped her wrist across her eyes. This wasn't his problem. She'd thought at first that they should talk it through, but now it was a gift she wanted to give him.

"I won't just quit there. I have to make sure there's someone to take over."

"Of course you do. I know it'll be hard to replace you. A lot of those ladies are pretty spry, though. Maybe they could do the cooking and cleaning."

"That's true. Some of them can work circles around me." She thought fondly of their busy hands and wisdom.

"So, they'll find someone. Maybe they could even run it as a co-op."

"Well, they already help, or I could never manage dinner for twenty-five people every day. But there's a lot more to it than just cooking and cleaning. There's fund-raising and a lot of government paperwork to qualify for the financial aid we get. Some of it gets pretty complicated."

Michael waved his fork. "Maybe you could do the paperwork for a while—maybe work on that from the café. But I really need you if we're going to hope to keep the café open all day. We'll have our own family business." He set his fork aside and slid his hand across the table to clasp hers. His warmth and strength helped settle her. "I like that. Us together as a team."

The tears no longer threatened as she looked into his bright eyes. "Yes, doing the book work from the café could be a temporary solution."

"Good, because I'd like you to be available to work at the café right away. Two weeks' notice is all anyone can ask, and even that is more tradition than ethical. It's a dog-eat-dog world out there. Most businesses expect their employees to move on with very little notice."

"I've always thought it was common courtesy to give an employer time to make adjustments." It crossed Jeanie's mind that her new employer was, in effect, her husband. She spoke a bit sharply when she added, "Any decent *new* employer would respect that."

Displeasure cut a furrow across Michael's forehead. His hand, resting gently on the back of hers, tightened. "If you're talking about me, I'm not your *new employer*. We're *partners*. I thought that was what you wanted."

Fear twisted in Jeanie's stomach. It was mild, a reflex really, left over from the old days. When Michael first came to town, she'd have used it as an excuse to whack him with the bat. But that wasn't right for them now. She didn't fear her husband. But she did respect him, and what she'd just said was rude. Who could blame him for being annoyed?

She turned her hand over and wove her fingers through his. "It *is* what I want. I'll get it all straightened out as soon as possible."

Michael nodded, satisfied, then let go of her hand and went back to his meal.

Her food grew cold as she worried at that fear. Michael had never laid a hand on her, ever. He'd done all his damage with words, cutting insults, tiny at first, then bigger and crueler. She let that worry morph into fretting about her friends at the nursing home and the senior center. The truth was she worked dirt cheap and worked hard. And both places scraped along, just like the library and the mini-mart. It wasn't a prosperous town. They were going to have a hard time replacing her.

"Why aren't you eating?" Michael picked up his plate and carried it to the kitchen sink.

Jeanie shrugged. "It was hard today. I loved working for those people, and they need me. I feel guilty abandoning them. I guess it killed my appetite."

Michael snagged his chair, moved it next to her, and sat down. "Well, don't skip too many meals." Michael grinned at her. "If you get any skinnier, you'll blow away."

"I thought you liked me skinny."

"I like everything about you." Michael lifted her onto his lap.

She squeaked in surprise then wrapped her arms around his neck, glad he was happy with her again. Yes, he liked everything about her, except her jobs and her volunteer work—the things that gave her a feeling of self worth. And her skinny body. He'd had a real problem with the weight she'd gained after Sally was born. So he didn't like her skinny and he didn't like her fat.

She had a split second to consider calling him on this strange, mildly hurtful conversation. He'd told her he wanted to be held accountable. But he was smiling, and she didn't want him to stop. And then he was kissing her, reassuring her with his touch that he liked her very much. And she definitely didn't want him to stop that.

He'd been so sweet about waiting until she was ready to make their marriage a real one, but she felt his frustration, and that deepened her guilt. But she still wasn't ready. Michael would just have to be patient.

One of his very worst skills.

thirteen

Jeanie had her hands full controlling her inner battle-ax. But she was careful not to become a nagging shrew of a wife.

Michael returned to his cheerful self. Of course, she tried hard to be loving and give him the respect due any husband.

The senior center surprised her by deciding to close when she resigned. Feeling terrible about it, they announced they'd all come to her restaurant for their noon meal, and some of them for breakfast and dinner, too. The community Meals-on-Wheels program had been attached to the senior center, so Jeanie continued providing those meals, and local volunteers delivered them just as they always had, only now they worked out of Jeanie's Café.

There was paperwork to do to transfer the government part of the subsidized program to a new address, along with the usual accounting. Michael agreed, somewhat grudgingly, to give a senior discount that equaled the very low price the Cold Creek retirees had been paying at Golden Days.

It made the café the center of the town's activities and brought attention to his rapidly expanding row of cabins. After the success of the rented Buffalo Bus on Memorial Day, Michael had found a shabby but functioning bus and bought it. He'd had signs attached to the side so they had an official Buffalo Bus and could run rides whenever a group asked for them.

Michael came into the café one hot day in the middle of June, exuberant. "We're building a golf course."

Jeanie looked up from her book work. She now did the books for the senior center, Meals-on-Wheels, the café, craft shop, and cabins as well. Michael had offered to do it, but she'd insisted. It had seemed like a matter of honor that she not turn over all the money to him, but she regretted taking on so much work that Michael would have done joyfully.

She really wasn't book smart. She was reminded of that daily as she struggled at her computer to make her account columns balance.

"A golf course?"

"Yeah, it was Jake Hanson's idea. There's a nice plot of land, too rough for much else, on the south side of town. He's getting a group together to do the work themselves. Did you know Jake is rich?"

"I guess I never thought about it. He doesn't live a fancy life."

"He's loaded. I'm going to encourage him to keep investing in this Cold Creek revitalization project. He sounds willing. He's excited about the golf course."

"Can you do that? Build a golf course yourself?" Jeanie knew nothing about golf, and that was the plain truth.

"Sure you can. It's mainly working with the contours and hazards already there and planting grass. Jake has the farm equipment, and we've got lots of people who can pitch in. It'll be rough at first, but that'll make for a challenging course. And I want to open up the garage bay on this place. Make it a bait and tackle shop, maybe carry some camping equipment. You've got the back room full of crafts, and I think we need to move them to the abandoned building next to the city offices on Main Street."

"Open another business?" Jeanie glanced at her mangled efforts at bookkeeping, wondering if she was up to it.

Mayor Herne rushed into the café, his face flushed pink from the summer heat. He pulled out a handkerchief and mopped his brow. "This golf course will be great. If we throw a lot of effort into it, we could seed the grass in September and possibly have it open for the late fall. There are several schoolteachers who aren't busy this summer who offered to do a lot of the heavy labor, cutting a fairway through a stand of trees here and there."

Jeanie didn't speak up about her worries over the craft shop or the bait and tackle. Heaving a sigh of relief that the golf course wasn't her problem, she went back to her figuring.

Michael and Bucky talked. A few more people came in, excited about the course. Jake came in carrying pictures of his baby, and he divided his time between fatherly pride and a long suppressed love of golf.

"I wish you'd brought Emily in, Jake. I haven't been out yet with a meal. I get lonely for her." Emily had been the best support in this last year. She was steady, sensible. Buffy was, too, but she had the same scars from her childhood that Jeanie had. And she had her hands really full. Plus Jeanie felt like such a failure around Buffy, no matter how kindly Buffy treated her.

Michael offered to design a simple clubhouse, and several of the men owned golf carts. They kept them in Hot Springs at the country club, the nearest place to play. But they offered to rent them out for people wanting to get from the cabins to the shops uptown to the golf course.

Jeanie listened with part of her attention while she did her figuring. Michael and his enthusiasm had caught fire yet again. She wanted to smile. She also had a twinge of concern that the local people were taking on too much, maybe donating more than they could afford.

With a mental shrug, Jeanie typed on until the crowd got agitated with a need to act and they all scrambled out the door, heading toward the future Cold Creek Links.

Jeanie spent another hour on her books then walked out to the nursing home to spend some time with her hospice patients. The outlook was bleak for both the patients, as was always the case, but one, Pete Hillman, had his family called in and wasn't expected to live through the night. Sadness hung heavy in the air. Jeanie spent a long while with Pete's two sons and their elderly mother as they discussed details of a funeral and all the complications involved in a loved one's death.

Her other hospice person, Janet Lessman, was in nearly as fragile a condition, and the elderly woman had her husband sitting faithfully by her side for hours every day. They had time for a brief visit and some prayer before she left.

By the time she walked home, it was well past time for dinner.

She came inside to find Michael striding back and forth. He looked up as if he'd been afraid she was dead. "Where have you been?" He was at her side in an instant.

"I was visiting at the manor. You know I spend a few evenings a week out there. One of my clients is dying."

"I thought they were all dying. I thought that's what hospice was all about."

With a sad nod, Jeanie said, "That's right, but the time is really close for Mr. Hillman. His family had a lot of questions and just needed someone there to handle the details."

"Okay, I'm sorry." He hugged her. "You worried me."

"Did you call the nursing home or anywhere else to check on me?"

"No, I haven't been home that long. But I was late, so I knew you were late." He pulled her closer. "I'm sorry. It just. . .it reminded me of the time we spent apart. I just kind of freaked out. Panicked. I was going to call 911 in about two minutes." He laughed.

She felt him shake his head against her neck. She felt the tremors. He'd really been worried. She lifted her arms to hold him, comfort him.

"Can you just leave a note next time if you're going to be

late? Something." Michael gave another shaky laugh. "I'm sorry. It's like I'm a parent worried about a kid who missed curfew. If you'd put your schedule on the refrigerator, it would give me a place to start looking."

Jeanie hugged him hard then pulled away. "Or a reminder that you don't need to start looking." She ran both hands into his hair, pushing it off his forehead. Then she pulled him down and kissed him. "Yes, I'll put the schedule up. It's a lot simpler now, without the work hours. And both the choir and my Tuesday Bible study are on summer break. Girl Scouts, too. I haven't been helping with the 4-H Club like I should, so I've kind of let others take over for the county fair, which is next week. So I'm pretty free these days, except for running the café and the bait and tackle store and the craft shop."

"I asked Bucky to find someone to take over the tackle store. I hope that's okay. I mean, how would you know what to order for tackle? Bucky knows an area fisherman or two who know just how they'd like things to be. And two of your seniors are going to run things for the craft shop."

Jeanie concealed a sigh of relief. "That's good. The café is keeping me really busy."

Feeling impish with so much weight off of her shoulders, she asked, "So, what are you making me for supper?"

Catching her face in both hands, Michael kissed her with a comic smack. "I'll be glad to make supper for my runaway bride. Let me see, what do I know how to make? Uh. . .cold cereal? No wait, do we have hot dogs?" He strode toward the kitchen. Glancing back, his eyes shone with mischief. "Do they have to be hot, or can we just eat them right out of the package?"

Jeanie caught up with him and shoved him playfully. "Forget it. I'm not trusting you within a mile of something I'm going to put in my stomach. I'll cook."

Stumbling for just a step, Michael grabbed her as if to

keep his balance and began tickling her. Laughing, she tried to escape, but he pulled her back, the tickling making her squirm and laugh like a loon.

"Stop." Jeanie finally yelled through her giggling. "I give. You win."

"Just remember who's bigger next time you make me worry." Michael left the kitchen. "Call me when dinner's ready. I've got some phone calls to make."

Too tired to get fancy, Jeanie put a couple of hamburgers in the skillet and warmed a can of vegetables; then she turned her attention to writing up her schedule as Michael had asked. It was different having to consider him. She thought they'd talked about all of her commitments, and heaven knew she'd dropped a lot of them, but he didn't have it all straight. A quick thrust of impatience had her thinking of all the details he juggled with his many projects, but somehow he couldn't remember that Jeanie visited hospice patients?

As she wrote, she realized just how many things she'd dropped in the two months since he'd been back. She'd even told the hospice organizer that she didn't want to be assigned any more clients, and Michael had found someone else to clean the church and weed the flower beds.

She was left with Monday morning church services at the nursing home, two quickly failing hospice patients, and some substitute piano playing at church. Michael was wheedling for her to do that only when absolutely necessary, because he wanted her to sit with him. As it was, she'd started coming down from behind the piano between songs.

She knew he chafed at her resuming her involvement with the Girl Scouts and the 4-H Club. She'd already told the other leaders that she wouldn't be available much from now on.

She had gone from busy all day every day to working about three hours a week outside the café. She tapped the paper as she studied it. Three hours, and Michael couldn't keep that straight? Her jaw tightened. How had this happened? He'd done some pushing, but she'd mostly just assumed he'd want her to quit. Actually, he'd been quiet about it, but she'd gotten the message.

Was this something she should bring up as part of being honest in her new marriage?

God, is it?

It wasn't comfortable, this total giving up of everything she was in order to be Michael's devoted wife. But she was still busy with the café and the book work she did.

The Bible verse about courage she had taped on her mirror at her tiny apartment was still there. She hadn't brought it along, but she had it memorized.

"We want you to be very strong, in keeping with his glorious power. We want you to be patient. Never give up. Be joyful."

Where was her strength? All residing in Michael's hands.

Yes, she had been patient, but was it the patience of strength, or was it just the quiet nature of a quitter, a coward?

Had she given up? It didn't feel like it, but it had been so incremental.

"Be joyful." She was happy in her marriage. Michael wasn't the tyrant he'd once been. Or was he? Was he even aware that he'd taken over Jeanie's life completely? And didn't a husband have the first claim on his wife's time?

God had even been pushed out of the center of her life. They prayed together over meals, but Jeanie hadn't had her quiet time with the Lord in the early mornings for a while. After they'd moved, she'd just never gotten back in the habit.

Should I challenge Michael on this?

In prayer, she listened for the leading of God. Instead of God's voice she heard Michael talk in the room he'd converted into an office. The words weren't audible, but the rising and falling of his salesman voice was clear.

For some reason, listening to that persuasive cadence made

her look around her kitchen for her bat. She hadn't seen it for a while. Odd that she suddenly wished for it.

Turning the dinner down, she hunted for her Bible and had a crushing sense of guilt that it took her many long minutes to find it, neatly tucked in a bookshelf.

She brought it with her to the kitchen and realized that the hamburgers had gotten too brown. Turning them off, she used a spatula to set them on a plate with the cold clink of metal on glass.

"Michael, dinner is ready." She'd read later.

"I'm almost done. I'll be right there."

Jeanie almost smiled at those familiar words. How many times had she held supper for him? He always had just one more call. She looked at the hamburger. Not burnt, but a bit crisp on one side. And the vegetables, one glance told her the green beans had cooked until they were mushy.

Michael would notice this. She almost rushed to the pantry closet for a new can of beans. If he delayed much longer, she'd be able to have a new hamburger cooked for him. She had some frozen, and with the microwave to thaw it—

She caught herself. "No. He'll eat it and be nice about it. Or he won't and I'll call him on it." Jeanie put a hamburger on Michael's plate and a serving of beans, then made a plate for herself and set it aside.

His voice continued in the background.

"It's getting cold, Mike."

"Just hang on another couple of minutes." He went on talking.

She sat down and opened her Bible. She'd marked verses about courage. She needed the kind of courage that she found only in the Lord. Because if Michael came in here and said one thing about the dinner or about her being late or too busy, she was going to stand up to him. And if he didn't take that well, she was moving out.

God, do I need to stand up for myself? Or am I just creating conflict in my home?

Prayerfully, she read her marked pages, trying to decide if she was willing to end up, before the night was over, alone in her little apartment.

fourteen

Michael hung up the phone, satisfied with the plans in place for the Fourth of July.

The Rapid City media was playing up the buffalo herd. Michael had placed some stories here and there about the fishing in Cold Creek and the small town charm. The cabins had been full every weekend since they'd opened, and he'd had enough weeklong reservations to make the place profitable, but it could do a lot better. They needed some hiking trails, maybe hook-ups for campers.

His mind busy, he went to the kitchen and found Jeanie reading at the table. His dinner was served and ready for him. Leaning down to kiss her cheek, he saw the Bible and his heart warmed. "You're wonderful, you know? I'm so glad we're together again."

She lifted her chin, and their lips met. She closed the Bible, set it aside, and pulled her plate into place. Michael sat next to her. Their hands clasped, then he pulled her close and they turned to God in prayer.

When they'd finished, they ate supper. Michael made no unkind mention of the pathetic meal.

Michael slid both their plates aside when they were done, and he picked up her Bible. "What were you studying when I came in for supper?" He flicked his finger over the row of bright pink sticky notes on the top of the book.

Jeanie smiled up at him, her gift of sunlight to him. Michael prayed silently as she took the Bible and flipped it open at one of the tiny stickies. "I've marked all the verses I can find about courage. It's been my one constant quest. I'm a coward. I've done terrible things out of fear." She flipped open the book to Colossians. "I've claimed this as my life verse."

Michael read. "I recognize this from our bathroom mirror at the apartment."

"Paul writing a letter of encouragement to the Colossians." Jeanie's graceful hand slid down the page to rest by the first verse. " 'We want you to be very strong, in keeping with his glorious power. We want you to be patient. Never give up. Be joyful.' All of this was missing in my life on the day I gave up Sally. I ran away, hitched a ride, and ended up in Denver. I'd stolen money from Buffy. I left feeling like. . ." Jeanie's eyes fell closed, and she shook her head.

"Like what, honey?" Michael sat around the corner from her. He scooted his chair so he was by her side and slid his arm around her shoulders, wishing his physical support could provide emotional support.

"Like I didn't deserve to live." She rested her head on his chest. "I felt so awful, just worthless. The bus station in Denver. . .I just walked out of it with no idea where to go from there."

She took a deep breath. "I saw a homeless shelter. There was a sign asking for volunteers. I still had some money but not that much. It was late, and I was in a bad neighborhood. I had no idea where to find a motel. I went in intending to help and get a meal in exchange, maybe even a place to sleep. I ended up staying for six months."

"In a homeless shelter?" Michael's skin crawled as he thought of the dangerous people who would inhabit such a place. He rubbed her shoulder as he imagined the filth and the bad food and the—

"I found God in that place. The man running the mission was a beautiful Christian. The kitchen had several people in it who had pretty much walked in off the street like

I had. They were wonderful, accepting." Jeanie gave a short, humorless laugh. "They'd all done things as bad or worse than I had. They were so shorthanded and thrilled with my offer to help. They—they needed me." Her voice faded to a whisper, as if being needed was beyond her imagination. Jeanie closed the Bible gently and hugged it. "I don't know if anyone had ever needed me before."

"I need you, Jeanie." He pulled her close, hugging her, the Bible between them. It felt so right.

Please, God, create something new in me. Give me the words to encourage her.

"No, you don't."

He looked down and saw the top of her head. So familiar, so much time in her short life with her head bowed in fear or shame. So much of it his fault.

"You *want* me for whatever reason." She spoke into his chest. "Or maybe you're just *stuck* with me and trying to figure out how to make it work. But you don't need me at all."

Michael gently lifted her chin until she looked at him. Tears coursed down her cheeks. Misery etched lines into her face.

God, forgive me. Help me. I never wanted to make her cry again.

He loved her. He couldn't resist lowering his head and kissing her. Even that, in the midst of her misery, she accepted and gave without thought to herself.

When the kiss ended, Michael said, "I think we've been too busy lately, running in so many directions. We need to be spending time with the Lord. A devotion every day. Tonight we start. Let's go through these sticky notes and read your verses. And we'll make time for the Lord every morning. We've been neglecting counseling, too. Let's ask Pastor Bert if we can meet with him once a week. Maybe he'll give you a new bat."

Jeanie laughed through her tears. "I think the bat actually helped. Even just sitting in the room it was a reminder to both of us that we had a weakness in our marriage that needed our constant attention." She stretched up and kissed him. "I'll tell you something that I probably shouldn't because it will just inflate your ego."

Michael widened his eyes in mock excitement. "I could really use this. You've reminded me of how far we have to go. My ego could use some inflation."

With another laugh, she said, "I'm so proud of you."

The mock excitement died, replaced with a melting heart. "You are?"

"You have so many great qualities. I have you close, and I start depending on you and obeying you because you're so smart and so full of life and enthusiasm. It's so logical that I'd let you lead. Mostly, ninety-percent of the time it would be stupid to do things any way except yours."

"Only ninety-percent?"

"Okay, ninety-nine percent." She punched his arm playfully.

"But you lose yourself." It was in his nature to take charge. He had to fight it, even if it made sense for him to run things.

"And since it's my own fault, it's even harder to talk about." She looked up, and Michael saw tears brimming in her shining eyes. "It's my problem. Taking it to you just dumps more on you and makes me a burden." Her voice broke, and she buried her face against his chest.

"You're not a burden, sweetheart. And it's not your problem. I am as much at fault in our marriage as you. More, in fact. I was the one who was—and sometimes still is—unkind. You were just too nice to start throwing coffee mugs at my head. Guess which one of those is the worst?" Aching for her, he ran a hand down her hair and held her as she cried.

After a few minutes, she shook her head and cleared her

throat. "The few tiny things I'd like different are silly. I start mentally beating up on myself, and it's worse than anything you do."

Michael offered her a handkerchief. "Probably not."

Mopping her eyes, she laughed again, a husky laugh with a throat swollen from crying. "Just be patient with me, Michael. Give me a chance to figure out how to change and grow and give you what you need."

"Thank you. Thank you for trusting me enough to say that. You're such a good, sweet person." He kissed her. And her generosity was his.

After Jeanie had left him to his lonely bed, Michael took a moment to thank God then remembered they'd left the Bible in the kitchen.

He should go get Jeanie, and they should keep that commitment they'd made to have a devotional time every day. But his eyes were heavy and he was too comfortable. They'd spend time with the Lord tomorrow.

A small voice whispered inside his head not to put God off until later. His eyes popped open, and suddenly his exhaustion was lessened. He shoved the blanket back and pulled on his robe as he headed for the kitchen. He reached Jeanie's room and knocked.

"Yes?"

He heard tension in her voice. He spoke quickly before she could get the wrong idea.

"We forgot to have an evening devotion, honey. Are you too tired?"

"No, I'm not too tired. It's a good idea."

"I left my Bible in the kitchen."

Jeanie's door opened. Her face was clean scrubbed. Her hair mussed as if she'd been tossing and turning in bed. Her eyes shone with pleasure that he'd thought of this and come to her.

It was all he could do not to pull her close and kiss her. Something in her eyes told him that, right now, she'd welcome him.

"I—I'll meet you there then." She didn't move to get her own Bible.

Unable to resist, Michael grabbed a quick kiss then a slower one; then he forced himself to straighten away from her.

"Great." He moved on down the hall.

fifteen

Besides her normal work, Jeanie had to get a meal together for Jake and Emily, to welcome the new baby.

Their son, Logan, was beautiful. He reminded Jeanie painfully of all she'd given up. She missed confiding in Emily, but her friend was so busy, Jeanie couldn't impose.

Jake was floating around as if he'd been crowned king. He'd also found some rush of energy from fatherhood. With the help of a volunteer crew and some rented earth-moving equipment, he'd cleared the whole golf course and smoothed the rolling hills, ready to seed in the fall.

The Fourth of July celebration was coming at them like a freight train. The whole town was excited. Everyone was involved. Michael had yet to talk with Buffy and sign the adoption papers, but who could blame him?

He'd found another inflatable bat, and Jeanie kept it behind the counter at her café, but she was too much in love to use it. They'd found posters and figurines of buffalo as well as some Western décor. Michael had insisted on offering buffalo burgers on the menu, although Jeanie knew Buffy hated the idea, and he'd had a sign made naming the place the Buffalo Café.

He didn't consult Jeanie about the sign, just presented it to her as a gift. He'd been calling it Jeanie's Café up to now. She'd enjoyed having it named after her for some dumb reason. Why would her name sell food?

Michael had hinted at doing the book work, and though that perturbed her and she'd teased him about the bat, he'd taken it over and she didn't miss doing it.

To thank him for helping, she decided to decorate *herself* a bit and had some highlights added to her hair and started wearing a little bit of makeup again. She'd really let herself go since they'd been apart.

The café and Jeanie were both beginning to shine.

"It's this weekend." Michael came home later these days, and Jeanie had remembered some old recipes that kept well on low heat. She'd quit offering him skimpy dinners.

Smiling as he came in the kitchen, she said, "I can't wait. You've got everything ready. It's going to be huge success."

"This town is going to become a destination." He slid into his place at the table. "We're a great low-cost alternative for people wanting Mount Rushmore and the Black Hills. I've printed up some tourist information with all the places to drive in short trips. Everyone who comes to town over the Fourth will get one. We're going to have to add cabins. Maybe I could even interest a chain in selling me a franchise."

Jeanie hurried to set a platter of lean roast beef in front of him and quickly drained the new potatoes she'd cooked; then she added a plate of fresh sliced tomatoes. Michael had encouraged her to hire more help at the café, and now she got home right after lunch.

She should have dropped by the nursing home to visit with her last remaining patient, but instead, she'd driven to Rapid City to have her hair done and she'd wanted time to bake bread for supper. Tomorrow was Thursday, and the Fourth of July weekend began in earnest on Friday.

When Michael had everything in front of him, she settled into her own place on the opposite side of the rickety white Formica-top table.

After he'd eaten a few bites, he managed to look up. "I'm sorry. I'm eating like a hungry wolf, and I've barely spoken to you. I'm starving and this tastes great." Then his eyes focused. "Hey, your hair. I like it."

Her heart gave a little extra leap of pleasure. "I had it cut. Lightened a little, too."

"You look terrific. You drove into Rapid City today, didn't you?" He slid one hand over her hair and took a second to touch her dangling earrings playing peek-a-boo with her sassy, uneven cut.

She'd told him she was going to, but it must not have registered until he saw her new hairdo.

"Yeah, there's a hairdresser in the mall I'd heard a lot about. The local beautician has a tendency to burn hair to a crisp with bleach." She spent mornings at the café, but with the hired help there wasn't a lot left for her to do except greet people. Michael had hinted that she should dress a little better for the job. She'd started wearing a skirt and heels to act as hostess. The shoes killed her feet, which made it all that much easier to hand the reins over to her very competent help.

"I'd rather go with you when you drive in the city. The traffic is pretty heavy."

"I'd prefer it if you went with me, too. I haven't done much city driving. I don't need to go back for a while. Maybe after the Fourth we could visit Mount Rushmore." She'd never owned a car since she'd moved to South Dakota. Hadn't wanted one, hadn't been able to afford one. So Rapid City was intimidating.

Michael went back to his meal, filling her in on all the details of his day. When he finished eating, he headed straight for the office and his phone. He called over his shoulder as he left the room, "It was a delicious meal."

Jeanie watched him go. Their counseling sessions with Pastor Bert had been delayed for the last two weeks. They needed to get back to them. They hadn't done their daily devotions for a few days either.

She bit her bottom lip and tried to figure out how to remind Michael, but it just wasn't fair to dump this all on him when he was so busy. But how was standing here feeling drab and afraid to drive fair to her?

It wasn't. She had let things slip, and she needed to stand up for herself again.

Their marriage should come first. And it would—after the Fourth. Things would settle down then.

The time was almost up on those adoption papers, too. By the end of summer, if Michael hadn't formally protested, the adoption would go through with or without his signature. But until it was finished, Jeanie would worry. And she'd started ducking Buffy at church so she wouldn't have to see her sister fume.

As she cleaned up the kitchen, Jeanie heard Michael's voice, that rise and fall, his wheeler-dealer voice. Somehow it seemed as if he'd sold her a bill of goods, too, but wasn't that just her own sinful nature fretting, being dissatisfied?

She took her Bible and went to her room. She preferred to stay in there most evenings so she wouldn't have to see Michael and conjure up all the enthusiasm he expected for the changes he was making in Cold Creek.

Sometimes he came to her room and held her, trying to sell her on the idea that all was well and their marriage should cease to be platonic. It reminded her of when they were dating.

Hesitantly, feeling like a bother, she left her room and looked in on Michael, who was working on his computer. "Are you using the phone?"

He looked up, a trace of annoyance on his face for being disturbed. "No, but isn't it a little late to make a phone call?"

"It's just past nine. I think it's okay."

"Who are you calling?"

That bothered her. As if he was going to approve or disapprove of letting her make the call.

"Emily."

Michael nodded, which Jeanie assumed meant she had permission.

She took the handset off of its cradle. "I'll make the call out here so I won't distract you."

Settled back in her bedroom, sitting on the edge of her single bed, she dialed and Jake answered.

"Is Emily there? I mean, don't bother her if she's sleeping or got her hands full with Logan."

"No, she'll be glad to talk to an adult. She claims she's reverting to baby talk herself." Jake laughed.

Jeanie realized that Jake's little comment could have been taken as slightly insulting to Emily, but he sounded so kind. Did all husbands put their wives down? Did Jeanie just hear Michael's perfectly innocent words and twist them into something darker? Was all her unhappiness coming from her own warped mind?

"Hi, Jeanie. Thank you so much for calling. I'm desperate to talk to a grown-up." Emily laughed. Jeanie knew how happy Emily was with Jake.

"I'm coming out with dinner as soon as I can."

"Well, do it when you can stay awhile. I need to show off Logan to someone. He's so beautiful."

"I—I need to talk to someone about Michael."

There was a stretched moment of silence. "Has something happened?"

"No, well, kind of, not really. I— I drove to Rapid City today and got—got my hair colored." Jeanie waited, wondering if Emily could possibly read her mind. This would be so much easier.

"Did Michael order you to do it?"

Maybe Emily could read her mind a little.

"No, he's never said a word. It's me. I've just got this—this racket inside my head. Michael hasn't done anything wrong, but I feel like such a failure. An embarrassment."

"But he's never said a word?" Jeanie heard the doubt in Emily's voice.

"Well, nothing really critical. He wants me to dress better to hostess at the restaurant."

"Which you interpreted to mean you're a failure and an embarrassment."

"Why do I do this? It's not Michael's fault if I've got critical voices inside my head telling me I'm not good enough."

"Did you have those voices before Michael came back?"

"Well, yes, some."

"But they're a lot louder now, right?"

"A lot."

"But you don't think that's Michael's fault, right?"

"It doesn't seem fair to blame him."

"So you blame yourself." The silence stretched. At last Emily asked, "Do you want me and Jake to come in?"

"No! It's too late."

The silence returned as if Emily was trying to read the truth behind Jeanie's words.

"What you really need to do is tell Michael all of this. I think he's really trying, but if he doesn't know when his words hurt you, he can't change."

"But he's so busy."

"Too busy to be kind? Can anyone ever be that busy?"

"Things will let up after the Fourth of July."

"Don't wait until then to talk to him. Go talk to him now."

"He's doing book work."

"Whack his keyboard with your bat."

Jeanie pictured it then started to laugh. Just talking to Emily, speaking of her fears aloud, helped ease them. She'd be able to sleep now. "Maybe I will."

"If you're afraid to talk to Michael, that ought to tell you something."

"Yeah, it ought to. I'll be more honest with him."

"Don't twist what I've said into a criticism of your honesty, Jeanie."

"I'm not. I'm sorry."

Again there was silence. At last Emily said, "I'm going to be watching Michael. I'll give you until after the Fourth to deal with him, and then I might just show up with a *real* bat. And I promise I won't be taking my swings at you."

Jeanie laughed again. "Thanks, Em. It really helped to talk."

She didn't go talk to Michael that night. She heard him heading for bed just as she was going and decided to wait until he wasn't so tired.

Complaining always made her feel so guilty. What business did she have complaining when she was so far from perfect herself? She was lucky a man like Michael wanted her. Lucky *any* man would want her after what she'd done.

Settling into sleep, Jeanie asked God to forgive her for all her worrying when she'd made this mess out of her life. She was finally, really, fully able to love her husband.

Dear God, thank You so much for loving me. And thank You that Michael loves me.

It occurred to her to ask God to help her love herself, but she just couldn't. It was too selfish.

sixteen

Michael was obviously thrilled with the turnout for the Independence Day weekend.

Jeanie could see that the rest of the town was stunned. Not her, though. She'd expected Michael to make a huge success out of anything he tried.

He'd had his back slapped and his hand shaken a hundred times since the first car pulled up Friday morning.

The parade had been huge and flashy and stirring. Tourists lined the streets. The fireworks had been spectacular— Michael had seen to that. There was a hustle and bustle on Cold Creek's Main Street that added up to financial success for everyone in town.

By the time it was over, the cabins were rented for the rest of the summer and for a lot of weekends next year. A hunting and fishing magazine had sent a crew and were clearly excited about this untapped area for fall and spring outdoor sports.

The buffalo were a smash. Jeanie had seen her sister looking jubilant, because keeping the buffalo ranch financially sound was always tricky.

As the last car pulled out of Cold Creek midafternoon on Monday, the town leaders congregated in the Buffalo Café. Jeanie served coffee and donuts. Things were badly picked over thanks to hungry tourists.

Michael went from table to table, full of plans for the future. The whole café buzzed with excitement.

Jeanie brought coffee around and accepted kind words from her neighbors, too, though none of this was her doing.

"Jeanie, have we stripped all the cupboards bare in this place?" Michael smiled at her and slung an arm around her shoulder.

"I'm down to crackers and unopened cans of chili. Not exactly coffee break food."

Michael kissed her soundly.

She loved him so much when he was happy. If only she could keep him happy.

He reached for her hair and ran a gentle hand over it, tucking it behind her ears.

"I'm sorry. I've just been running all day. I must be a mess." Jeanie reached up to smooth her hair, wondering what it looked like. The pleasure of the day faded as she worried about shaming Michael. She saw that her nails were chipped. Her makeup must have melted off hours ago.

"You're fine. Stop worrying. Just go check in the mirror. Your mascara's a little smeared." Michael looked closer. "Or maybe you've got circles under your eyes. What an exhausting weekend for you."

"You, too."

"Yeah, but it's like caffeine in my blood. Being around people energizes me. You're happier when it's quiet."

"I've been happy this weekend. I've loved the activity."

Michael relaxed his hold. "Go check in the mirror, okay?"

Jeanie nodded and practically ran out of the room. There was a small restroom in the kitchen for the help. She went there and fussed with her appearance, dallying, wishing everyone outside would go away before she had to come out. She'd forgotten how much she hated crowds. When she'd been in the restroom for half an hour, she peeked out the door and saw that things had calmed down. She swung the door open and was surprised to see Buffy waiting in the kitchen, her arms crossed. Beside her stood Emily Hanson, with Logan, just a couple of weeks old, held close against her chest.

"We heard that." Buffy scowled and studied Jeanie's face as if she were a bug under a microscope.

"H–heard what?"

"What he said to you." Emily patted Logan's back. Emily had straight brown hair and sun-browned skin like Buffy. But Emily was taller. She was still rounded from having her baby. And Emily's eyes were kind, whereas Buffy glared with anger.

"Who?"

Buffy snorted. "How long did it take him to put you back in your place? He'd been here, what—two weeks, maybe a month?—before you quit all your jobs and started wearing too much makeup, trying to be good enough for that worthless Michael Davidson."

"He's not worthless. He's done so much for this town." Jeanie looked past Buffy's shoulders into the dining room, terrified Michael would overhear.

"He's gone. Relax. He won't *catch you* having an opinion. He hasn't done half for this town of what you did."

"Are you kidding? He built these cabins."

"He closed the senior center."

"They eat here now for the same price. And he brought tourists to your buffalo ranch."

"He's cut the hours the library is open."

"I didn't know about that." Jeanie rested one hand on her chest, surprised to learn of it. Keeping the library open as many hours as possible had been important to this town.

"Julia can't handle the extra hours, so she's just closing it for the evening hours."

"That's not Michael's fault." Jeanie needed to phone Julia. If there was no other way, Jeanie could go back to work. Except Michael wouldn't like it.

"The Russos are putting the mini-mart up for sale," Buffy added.

"They are?"

"Tim thinks it's too hard on their kids to work such long hours. He's hoping with the tourist rush he can unload the place on someone."

"Has he tried hiring teenagers? They usually need some spending money."

"There are three new patients at the nursing home that need hospice care. Someone is driving over from Hot Springs to take care of them."

Emily nudged Buffy, and the two of them exchanged another glance. Buffy rubbed her mouth as if she had to physically restrain the words.

Jeanie bristled. "I'm not the only person in this town who could be a hospice volunteer. Michael needs me."

Buffy's eyes narrowed, but she didn't speak.

Jeanie looked to Emily for support. Instead, she saw pity.

"Didn't you hear what he said to you, Jeanie?" Emily asked. "He's unkind."

"He told me I looked tired."

Buffy shook her head, her jaw tense. "Another way of criticizing you."

"No, a way of protecting me. He's taking care of me."

"It's not just that. I've watched him." Emily reached out and rested a hand on Jeanie's arm. "He puts one of his little barbs into you, and you start trying to fix it, make him happy. You've changed since he came back, Jeanie. You're not happy anymore."

"I wasn't happy before." Jeanie balled her fists. There was truth in what they said. And yes, Buffy had an old ax to grind, but Emily had no history with Michael.

"When you phoned me the other night, you said you'd deal with this after the holiday rush," Emily said. "Well, it's after."

Emily and Buffy exchanged a long look. Jeanie ached inside for being on the outside of whatever passed between these two. They were her best friends.

Then Buffy smiled. But the sadness in her eyes overruled the smile. "I want you to be happy, Jeanie." Buffy rested one of her work-roughened hands on Jeanie's arm.

Jeanie remembered all the times she'd sneered at Buffy for the hard, dirty work of wrangling buffalo. Jeanie patted Buffy's hand. "You know, don't you, that all those times I was such a brat to you when we were kids and after Michael left me came from jealousy?"

Buffy's forehead wrinkled. "Jealousy? You were the one who was cool. You had so many friends. You were popular."

"I was a C student, and you were a genius. I was superficial, and you had real depth."

"I was a geek, two years younger than anyone in my class. I walked the halls alone and ran out of school to work because I had no one to talk to."

"Not even me." Jeanie frowned. "Especially not me."

"I loved you, Jeanie. I understood how having your dorky, sullen, brainiac sister in class was embarrassing."

Jeanie looked at Emily. "Has she ever told you about when we first went to high school?"

"It doesn't matter now." Buffy squeezed Jeanie's arm and shook her head as if to warn her not to go on. "That's ancient history."

"We'd moved that summer. We moved around a lot."

"Don't talk about this, please." Buffy begged with her eyes as well as her words.

"I've never talked to you about it. Never apologized."

"I knew what you were going through."

Jeanie hugged Buffy. "That's perfect, trying to stop me from telling this. Just like back then. You've always tried to protect me. Even then you got it that I needed protection more—more than you did."

Jeanie's voice broke, but she steadied herself and went on, focusing on Emily. "We moved to Chicago. Dad worked for a manufacturing company that moved him around a lot. He claimed it was a promotion every time, but it wasn't. He was an accountant, but they'd transfer him from place to place because, I think, no one wanted to work with him for long."

"He'd been there long enough that they couldn't outright fire him, but I think they wanted him to quit," Buffy added.

"So we showed up at school and went our separate ways— Buffy to the gifted program, me to remedial classes."

"They weren't remedial. They were just normal courses."

"Maybe. It might have just felt remedial compared to you." Jeanie shifted away from her friends and went into the now-deserted café seating area, talking as she went. "I was, of course, immediately popular. I just knew all the moves, how to laugh, how to cozy up to the right crowd, how to dress and flirt and draw attention to myself for all the shallowest reasons."

"You were beautiful then, just like you are now." Buffy followed her.

Jeanie started wiping off the tables, and Buffy grabbed a rag while Emily bounced her sweet baby.

"So, I never acknowledged Buffy. No one knew I even had a little sister."

"And I hadn't talked to you either. We didn't run in the same circles."

"We were in the lunchroom one day. I saw her sitting by herself."

"Not even at the brainiac table. I was always antisocial." Buffy smiled at Emily. "I did homework during lunch, because after school I hung around at a wild animal park in Chicago so I could be near buffalo. I was one of those people who, if I'd snapped and done something crazy, everyone who knew me would have said, 'Yeah, we knew she was a troubled, crazed loner. Yeah, she kept to herself, too quiet.'"

Jeanie laughed. "They would not have."

"I thought you were from Oklahoma," Emily said.

Buffy shrugged. "We were from everywhere and nowhere. We came to Cold Creek from Oklahoma."

Logan started fussing. Emily settled on a chair near the center of the room as the sisters cleaned, straightened chairs, and talked.

"So this day at lunch, one of the *real* crazed loners at the school came up to the table where Buffy was sitting and started hassling her. 'You're in my seat. Beat it shrimp.' Stuff like that, shoving her."

"I *was* a shrimp. Small for my age, plus two years ahead of my grade level. I was twelve in the middle of a bunch of fourteen-year-olds, and smart as I was, I had a gift for making sure people around me knew I was smarter than they were. I was obnoxious. I didn't fit in at all. I never should have skipped those grades. It made everything harder."

"Buffy got up to move, but the guy knocked her tray as she stood, and it splattered all down her front. Milk and some kind of pudding and some gravy or something, really messy. And the whole place started to laugh."

"That guy got in big trouble. I got even."

"And she looked up, her clothes ruined, people laughing at her, and she looked right into my eyes, even though I was across the room."

"Jeanie, it's okay. It's over."

"And she needed me." Jeanie's voice broke. She breathed slowly, regaining control before she went on. "She needed help. There I sat at that table full of cheerleaders and jocks. If I'd had the guts to go to her, to bring my friends along, we could have protected her."

"You were afraid. I understood."

"You understood that you were completely alone." Jeanie stopped wiping her tears with her hand and fished a tissue out of her apron pocket to wipe her eyes. Then she tucked it away and braced both her hands flat on the table and looked squarely at Buffy. "On your own. Dad wouldn't stop hassling you for being so different."

"He hassled you, too."

"Mom wouldn't stand up for anyone against him."

"You included."

"The school kids picked on you."

"I got good at avoiding them. I always had a healthy knack for self-preservation."

"The way you looked at me, Buffy. Inside that brave, lonely shell you'd built around yourself, you needed me and you saw that I was not going to rescue you."

"You couldn't have."

"That my shallow friends were more important to me than my own sister, my own flesh and blood."

"Jeanie, don't. It's over."

"You looked at me as if I'd. . .I'd stabbed you in the heart." Jeanie's tears spilled again, and she fumbled for the tissue.

"No." Buffy set her cloth aside and came to Jeanie.

"Yes. I don't think you meant to let me see I'd hurt you. I think consciously you knew better than to expect anything of me. But you stood there dripping, being laughed at, so humiliated, and I. . .I picked up my tray, got up, and turned away. I left. I didn't even stay to see what happened next or if you had to wear those messy clothes the rest of the day."

Buffy put her arms around Jeanie, and Jeanie grabbed hold of her little sister—who was inches taller than her—and held on to her, too late, too much harm done.

"I love you, Jeanie. I do. I've forgiven you."

"I can't forgive myself."

Emily came up beside them. "You have to, Jeanie. It's so long ago. We all did stupid things at that age. And I'm sure Buffy was a major embarrassment. I can totally see pretending not to know her."

"Hey!" Buffy whacked at Emily.

Emily dodged, which wasn't hard, because Buffy wasn't trying to hit her. "Be careful of the baby!" Emily's mock offended cry calmed Jeanie's tears.

Shifting away from Buffy, Jeanie gave up on her soggy tissue and snagged a paper napkin out of the stainless steel holder on the table beside her, dabbing her eyes. She knew they were trying to lighten the mood. "Maybe if that's the only stupid thing I'd done, it wouldn't cut so deep. But I spent my whole life doing stupid things. Like abandoning Sally."

Buffy patted her, and Jeanie knew, even now, she was taking more than she was giving. Buffy had always been the strong one.

"You did the right thing for Sally. You weren't able to take care of her. Leaving and finding God, finding yourself, were things you needed to do. You're stronger now, a good Christian woman that I'm proud to have as a friend and a sister."

"Thanks. I'm trying to give enough to make up for the harm I've done."

"That's not how it works, Jeanie." Emily gave her a quick one-armed hug. Logan cooed, and he was close enough to Jeanie's ear that she heard that perfect sweet innocence. "God forgives even though we *don't* deserve it. We forgive others, even though *they* don't deserve it. Why do you have to earn the right to receive forgiveness from yourself? I don't believe God asks that of us."

The baby whined, and Emily started a maternal bouncing that Jeanie recognized. She'd held Sally like that. And she'd given Sally up. A mother's most basic instinct is to protect her child, to fight and even die for her child, and Jeanie had walked away, just as she'd walked away from Buffy all those years ago. A coward. A weakling.

"We want you to be very strong, in keeping with his glorious power. We want you to be patient. Never give up. Be joyful."

"He asks us to start fresh." Emily pulled Jeanie out of her self-inflicted pain. "Yes, if you have wrongs you can right, I believe you should do it. But to still hate yourself for knowing you weren't able to take care of Sally? To still hate yourself for being self-centered in high school? C'mon, Jeanie, you're a decent, hardworking, generous, loving woman. Everyone who knows you loves you. It's time to learn to love yourself."

Jeanie nodded. "I know that's true. I know God washes us clean and lets us start again. But just because it's true, doesn't make it easy to accept."

The baby turned up his whine to a cry, drawing the attention of all three women. "He's hungry. I want to get him home before I feed him so he'll take a good nap." Emily smiled sheepishly. "I'm trying to get him on a schedule, but I've been running around so much, he can't settle into anything."

"Thanks for taking the time to talk, Em." Jeanie waved her off.

Buffy headed for the door behind Emily. As she left she looked back. "I don't think you see it, Jeanie, but you *are* letting Michael talk down to you, insult you. It's not much, just little things, but I'm afraid you'll let him go back to being a tyrant just because you feel like you deserve to be abused. If you can't believe you deserve better, then how about you believe *Michael* deserves better. I can tell he's a changed man, a better man, even though the big, dumb jerk has yet to sign those adoption papers. But he could backslide into the tyrant he once was if you let him, and that's bad for him as well as you."

Buffy's words hit home. "You're right. He asked me to hold him accountable. I've been failing at that." Jeanie nodded. Just another failure. "I'll talk with him about it tonight."

"Good." Buffy gave her chin a firm jerk of satisfaction and left, the doorbell jangling overhead.

Jeanie stood alone in the tidy diner and wished she had as much confidence in her entire body as Buffy showed in that single nod.

seventeen

That night at supper, Jeanie wanted to bring up all that Buffy had said.

She couldn't.

Michael was flying from the success of the holiday weekend and bubbling over with plans for Labor Day and to make Cold Creek a year-round tourist mecca.

She did decide, though, to be brave and ask a few questions that had her worried. "You know, Mike, Cold Creek is a little town. You've been getting a lot of volunteer work out of the citizens here, and a lot of the ones who've helped most are retired. They're the ones with the spare time."

Michael cut through the savory, steaming lasagna with his fork.

Jeanie had used cottage cheese and a jar of store-bought sauce. Michael preferred ricotta and the sauce Jeanie made from scratch, but the local grocery store didn't carry the more exotic cheese and she didn't have access to fresh oregano and basil. The salad was poured out of a prepared bag of greens. The dressing was bottled. She braced herself for his cutting comments, but he ate with apparent relish.

"The community support has been terrific. I'm starting on a new cabin tomorrow. I've got room for five more cabins, and I'm building a footbridge across Cold Creek. A rope bridge I think. It'll look like something out of an old jungle movie, but it needs to be sturdy. I'll find some plans on the Internet and order the supplies. Jake Hanson said he'd—"

"My point is," Jeanie cut him off, feeling very powerful, "that you may be asking too much from these elderly people."

"Jake isn't elderly."

"Don't pretend like you don't understand what I'm saying." Jeanie refused to flinch when he narrowed his eyes at her tone. "My senior center folks are all retired. They've been working long hours every day on this project, and they've loved it. But expect them to wear out pretty soon and want their quiet life back."

Michael frowned. "I thing the town is committed to this renewal effort, Jeanie. I think they'll stick with me."

"They're excited about it, it's true. But most of your volunteers are one wrong step away from a broken hip. Oh, some of them are really spry, but a lot of them have serious health concerns. A few of them go south for the winter, and others don't get out much when the snow flies." Jeanie felt Michael's disapproval. He didn't like her contradicting him, but she remembered Buffy talking about Michael being critical and decided that if he said one wrong word, she'd hunt up her bat and have at him.

"I think you need to assess the progress and start thinking in terms of making them real paying businesses. If we hired someone and paid a living wage, the employee might relocate to Cold Creek. A young man maybe, with a wife and kids. Maybe several of them eventually. That would be *real* renewal, new families, new homes, a real estate market, a growing school system."

Michael nodded. "That will happen, but the profit margin is pretty slim right now. I want to get more of the investment recouped before I raise the operating costs."

She let out a muted sigh of relief. He wasn't going to criticize. He was listening and debating. She rested her hand on Michael's and smiled. "Just so you have it in mind and understand when your work crew starts dropping out to play cribbage."

"I stand warned." Michael nodded. "I've got rental agreements for Labor Day weekend for six cabins that don't exist.

Tomorrow I start building. You're right about the volunteer help. I've been donating a lot of money to this. Several others, like Jake, have, too, but it needs to be a paying concern. And if I have to start paying for labor. . ." He tapped the table thoughtfully.

"Well, I can build these six cabins myself. Maybe a few more. They're such a simple design. I'll set up the foundations tomorrow then pour cement the next day. Then start framing." Michael finished his dinner. "This was good, honey. I haven't had a real meal in a long time. Just one more way I was an idiot."

He helped her clear the table and for once didn't have a dozen phone calls to make. He stayed and dried the dishes while she washed. He asked questions and nudged her with his elbow, grinning, if she didn't answer him quickly enough, until she got fed up with him. Still feeling the power that had come earlier when she'd disagreed with him and he'd listened, she retaliated for his next nudge by splashing dishwater on him.

"Hey!" He shoved the plate he'd just dried into the cupboard and turned on her. "Of course you know this means war!" He slung his dish towel around her waist, grabbed both ends, and pulled her close.

Giggling, Jeanie reached for the water again.

"Got to get you away from the dangerous water weapon." He dragged her a few feet from the sink.

She leaned back for the water, and he dropped the towel and put his hands on her waist to turn her fully away from her soggy arsenal. He gave her a slurpy kiss on the neck, making as much noise as possible, while she giggled and wrestled, screaming when the kiss began to tickle.

"Say you give up."

"Never!"

Michael's strong arms circled her and he lifted her off her feet. "You're helpless. Admit I'm a big, strong man and you're a helpless female."

"Give me my bat. Then we'll see who's helpless."

Michael let her go with a mock shout of fear. "Not the bat. No, I'll be good."

Jeanie leaned back against the sink, her face hurting from the laughter.

Michael sat on one of the kitchen chairs, smiling until it nearly split his face in two.

She loved him. She knew it was back, fully alive in her heart. Better this time, too. More honest, more of a partnership than their marriage had been before.

Michael looked around the shabby kitchen. "I've spent so much time focusing on work, but we need to fix this house up, too."

"We will eventually. For now, you need to finish drying these dishes."

"Yes, ma'am." His gaze settled on her as he stood and approached the sink. Nervous about the strange intent expression, she turned and pulled the plug on the sink. He finished putting the clean dishes away.

Jeanie wiped out the sink. "The house is old, but I like it. There's no rush with remodeling. Are you done with that towel? Can I use it?" Jeanie reached for the tissue-thin terrycloth in his hand, and when she pulled, he didn't let go. Instead, he let her pull him right into her arms.

She looked into his glowing eyes. He was so handsome it almost hurt. He leaned down and kissed her.

He'd been really sweet tonight. And respectful. She was figuring out how to finally be his wife. How to find from God the courage to make herself and Mike better people.

She kissed him back.

Seconds ticked by. Her arms went around his neck.

Minutes passed, he pulled her close.

"I've missed you," she whispered.

He kissed her forehead, her eyes.

He was her husband. She believed marriage vows were eternal. She'd missed him, but she hadn't realized how much until right now.

"I've missed you, too." Michael breathed the words against her neck. "And we're forever. Aren't we?" He pulled back to plead with his words and his expression.

The answer to his question was nothing more than the truth. She wouldn't deny it. "Yes, we're forever." She pulled him back into another kiss.

When it ended, Michael said, "I want this marriage to be a real one, before God, Jeanie. I'd like to say our vows again, with Pastor Bert there. And we'll be married—and all that goes with it."

She studied his intent, sincere expression. "Yes, I think I'm ready, but I want to make our vows before God, too. First."

"We'll talk to Pastor Bert tomorrow. Maybe we can have a wedding tomorrow night."

Jeanie smiled at his usual push to get things done his way and fast.

Jeanie remembered that feeling of power she'd had earlier and wanted to have some say in this decision. She didn't want to be rushed. "How about Saturday instead? Give me one more week, Michael. One more week to be ready to truly be your wife again."

He nodded. "Saturday it is."

He pulled her close and sealed their promise with a kiss.

eighteen

Michael had two more cabins framed by the end of the week.

He was so happy with his life that energy poured out of him and he worked like a hyperactive dynamo. He prayed with every rip of the circular saw, praising God for the rebirth of his marriage. He'd been elated the first time Jeanie had told him she loved him. Now his feet barely touched the ground.

Saturday. Pastor Bert had agreed. Michael had spread the word around town, and a few plans were quietly being made for a simple reception for anyone who wanted to attend. He was counting the minutes.

God, thank You, praise You. I love You. Thank You for giving my wife back to me.

The visitors in his cabins were an added pleasure. He'd been trying to ask less of his volunteers, grateful to Jeanie for pointing out his insensitivity. He liked doing it himself anyway. He ordered the supplies for the footbridge and was so excited about the project he had them overnighted at a ridiculous expense.

The supplies came in, and Michael threw himself into the project. He wanted the bridge up and available for the renters now vacationing in the finished cabins. It was a pretty thing—three-inch-thick synthetic rope that looked like jungle vine and the walking surface made of treated redwood planks.

The charm of it would be a draw, and the word of mouth would bring in repeat customers. Plus, he needed to start erecting cabins across the creek, and this bridge was an essential part of that, because it was a long way to the nearest bridge a car could cross to reach cabins on the other side. But his vacationers could easily roll luggage across the footbridge.

He'd ordered a kit containing all the material, so the heavy ropes, including solid rope sides more than waist high on an adult, were easy to hang. Jake helped Michael pour a cement foundation on both sides of the creek.

Jake's help was invaluable, and Michael liked the guy, but Jake was so gaga over his new baby that it reminded Michael of all he'd given up when he'd abandoned Sally. He'd been working so hard that he'd let things slide with the adoption papers. He'd never intended to sign them, but he hadn't dared to make that clear until things were settled with him and Jeanie. He needed to get this wedding over with; then he'd deal with the legalities of regaining custody. He wanted to do it right. Give Sally a chance to get to know him and Jeanie well before they brought her permanently home.

A twinge of guilt made him wonder how Sally would handle it. Buffy was the only mother Sally had ever known, from what Jeanie had said. And Sally was five now; that was pretty old to be moved out of someone's house. But it had to be done. Sally was his. He couldn't give up his daughter.

Jeanie was threading the heavy ropes through the predrilled redwood planks as Michael had instructed her. She was always right at hand, helping wherever she could.

Michael liked having her close a lot more than Jake. And she liked being close; Michael could tell. She was as eager for Saturday's recommitment ceremony as he.

God, I was such a fool not to enjoy her as she was before. Forgive me for the way I treated her. Help me be a better person.

Michael sat side by side on the ground with his wife. "We just need to tie each plank in place. Then we pull these ropes through the holes on those pylons across the creek." He pointed to the wooden posts, nearly a foot in diameter and eight feet tall. They came predrilled with steel reinforced holes for the top and bottom of the footbridge. "Then we tighten the rope, tie it off, and we're done."

She smiled at him as she worked, threading the rope like a pro. He marveled at what a great team they made.

"You're sure this will be safe?"

Michael nodded. "I've talked to a guy who put up a suspension bridge in five different places, including one near Mount Rushmore. In fact, he's going to mail me some pamphlets on his bridges that we can give out to our tourists, to tie Cold Creek more closely to Mount Rushmore. And the State Game and Parks Department is sending out an inspector as soon as the bridge is done, so before we let a single person walk across it, we can have an expert test it for safety. Our insurance company reduced our rates when I promised we'd do that."

"I've got my last plank tied down. I'm ready."

Michael turned and grinned at her. They were sitting cross-legged on the rough, grassy ground by the edge of the chuckling creek. Towering trees shaded them. Dappled sunlight winked through on the warm July day. Birds sang and the breeze made its own music as he counted his blessings.

He leaned over and kissed her. "I'm so glad I can do that. I'm so glad we're together again."

Jeanie reached up and laid a hand on his cheek. "I thank God for you every day, every hour. He's given me a miracle."

"He's given *us* a miracle, you mean." Michael's contentment was like nothing he'd ever experienced. He marveled at the blessings of a Christian life as he quickly finished his side of the bridge.

The tied-together wood weighed a lot. He had already moved his pickup to the other side of the creek. Once he threaded the rope to the anchors on the far side of the rippling water, he'd hitch the ropes to the pickup. He'd drive slowly forward, dragging the heavy bridge across the expanse.

"Great. I'll attach the four ropes here." Michael quickly secured the near side of the bridge. "Now I'll wade across with it and thread it through the eye of the brace on the far side."

Jeanie giggled as he pulled on hip waders.

"Hey, you think these are funny-looking, but they beat being soaked to the knee."

"I'm sure they do." She fought the laughter and lost.

Her laughter sent sunshine along as he worked down the steep banks of Cold Creek, across the gently murmuring rivulet of the shallow stream, and up the far side. He'd tied narrow ropes to the heavy ones, so he didn't have to deal with all the weight as he crossed.

Climbing up the other side, he scrambled to hold all four ropes and not lose his footing. The anchoring pylon was as solid as Michael's construction experience and Jake's engineering skills could make it, which amounted to it being very solid indeed.

Michael pulled the bottom two ropes through their appointed holes easily. The top ones were just a bit over his head, but he slid one into place and secured it then started for the other. Standing on his tiptoes, he held the pylon with one hand and the rope with the other. When he got the rope threaded, he released the wooden stake to grab the rope and felt his boots slip on the dampened concrete.

"Jeanie!" Michael flailed, grabbing to stop his fall. He caught the unsecured rope and pulled it over the edge of the creek with him.

As he fell, head-over-heels down the rocky slope, he heard Jeanie scream.

๑

Jeanie was running before he hit the ground.

"Michael!" She splashed through the water toward his still form sprawled at the bottom of the bank. She skidded to her knees as she approached him, to hear a soft groan. He was alive!

His face was covered in blood, his right arm twisted under him.

"Michael, can you hear me?"

His eyes flickered open then fell shut.

She hated leaving him, but after a frantic moment of indecision, she got up and ran back across the creek. She screamed the whole time.

Glynna emerged from the café before Jeanie got all the way up the side. "What is it? What happened?"

"Call 911! Michael has fallen. He's unconscious. He's on the far side of the creek." She whirled and ran back. Dropping to his side, she pulled off the overshirt she wore. Wadding it, she gently but firmly pressed it to the ugly gash on Michael's temple. Thinking of spinal injuries, she kept his neck from moving. What else? His arm was bent at an awful angle, but she didn't dare touch it.

She prayed. "Please, God, don't take him from me when I've just found him again."

Tears nearly blinded her.

Michael whispered, "Jeanie?"

"Yes, I'm here." She dashed her tears away, barely noticing her hands soaked in blood. She leaned close to his barely moving lips. "The ambulance is coming."

Even as she spoke the siren fired up only a few blocks away. "Help will be here in a few seconds."

He didn't respond.

An ambulance and a police car—Cold Creek only had one of each—pulled up as close to the far side of the creek as they could get.

Tim Russo, her boss from the mini-mart, was fire chief. He ran to the bank across from her and headed straight down. "We're bringing a stretcher across instead of going around." Tim approached her. "It will save a lot of time."

More people came dashing through the water, the first two carrying a stretcher. Behind them came someone with an armload of supplies.

Tim got there first and crouched beside Michael. "Did he fall from the top?"

"Yes." Jeanie looked up; the pylon towered overhead. It was probably twenty or thirty feet, but it seemed like hundreds from where she knelt. How bad could his internal injuries be? His spine?

"Has he been conscious?"

"He moaned, said my name." Her voice broke. "H he opened his eyes once for a second."

The rest of the team arrived, and Jeanie was gently but firmly moved aside. The rescue squad was well trained, and Jeanie watched, crying quietly as they stabilized Michael's neck and lifted him with skilled precision onto the stretcher. Someone put arms around Jeanie's shoulders, and she was barely aware of being guided along behind the paramedics.

When she settled into a car, she realized it was the mayor's wife, Carolyn, driving. "I'll follow the ambulance to the hospital. You shouldn't drive when you're so distraught."

"Thank you."

"We're going to stop and get you some dry clothes, too."

Jeanie registered only vaguely that she was soaked nearly to the waist and shivering, though mostly from fear rather than cold. "No, I want to be with him."

"Hush, honey. We'll still be there long before they let you see him. You know how emergency wards are. They're taking him to the Hot Springs hospital, and if they're even the least bit worried about severe injuries, they'll life-flight him. If you end up in Rapid City in wet clothes, you'll be miserable."

"Life-flight?" Jeanie started crying harder.

They pulled up to the house, and Carolyn didn't even ask

whether Jeanie wanted to help pick out clothes. She ran and was back with a small pile clutched in her arms within seconds. Her tires screeched as she pulled away from the curb and headed south out of town. In grim silence, broken only by Jeanie's sobs, they raced down the road. A siren sounded behind them before they'd gone a mile.

Jeanie looked up, afraid the police would pull them over, but Carolyn, in a move that would have made a NASCAR driver proud, had somehow arranged for a police escort. The police car pulled ahead of them, and Jeanie recognized Bucky driving. He wasn't on the police force. But he was mayor, and Cold Creek's police force, one full-time chief and two part-time deputies, were probably all on the rescue squad, so there'd been no one to drive along with Jeanie and clear the road.

As they tore down the winding highway, weaving and twisting through the rugged hills and forests, Jeanie prayed silently until Carolyn began praying aloud. They recited the Twenty-third Psalm together. Jeanie prayed her courage verses; she'd never needed them more.

A few of the turns were nearly hairpin, and Jeanie closed her eyes, but she didn't ask Carolyn to slow down.

They pulled up to the Hot Springs hospital just as a roar overhead told them that indeed a helicopter was coming to take Michael to Rapid City.

"What did they find? What did the rescue squad learn on the drive in?" Jeanie leaped out of the car.

Carolyn was beside her, hustling her toward the helipad.

The Cold Creek ambulance sat, siren still screaming, lights strobing, near the concrete pad.

"Thank you so much," Jeanie murmured through her fog of terror. "Thank you for getting me here."

She got to the ambulance as the helicopter settled in place. Tim swung open the doors, and two other men rounded the ambulance to help ease the gurney out onto the ground. An

IV bottle held aloft was carried along.

"Can she ride along, Tim?" Bucky yelled over the roar of the helicopter blade, his hand blocking the bruising wind.

Two people leaped out of the helicopter and came to meet them.

Tim stepped away from the gurney as the helicopter EMTs took over carrying it. "Yes, you ride with him. We've been on the radio to them. They know you're coming along, Jeanie."

Jeanie couldn't get close to Michael, but she caught a glimpse of his blood-soaked face, his eyes closed, his body strapped down.

Her knees buckled, and Tim and Bucky caught her before she collapsed and nearly carried her along.

"Thank you. Thank you so much."

The gurney wheels folded as they slid Michael, still unconscious, into the helicopter. Jeanie's arms were steadied as she was boosted in beside him. A formidable-looking black woman, with a name tag that said Shayla, towed her to a flight seat and clicked her into a seat belt. A bundle that Jeanie thought were the clothes Carolyn had fetched was settled near Jeanie's feet. There was barely room for Jeanie in this small helicopter. The little seat she occupied was probably for one of the rescue workers.

"Stay there. Don't make me sorry we let you ride along." Shayla's compassionate eyes didn't match her no-nonsense words and brusque movements.

Jeanie decided Michael was safe in this woman's hands.

The door slammed. Shayla left Jeanie and turned to her patient before Jeanie had a chance to promise to be good.

The helicopter took off. Jeanie felt her stomach stay behind as they lifted.

Please, Lord, don't take Michael from me. We've just found each other again. We could make a life pleasing to You. Heal him, protect him, bless him.

She focused on Michael to keep her mind off the swooping of the chopper.

Two people worked over him in the cramped space. The woman talked steadily. The other emergency worker, a dark-haired man with a ponytail, leaned over Michael's head. Both of them moved constantly.

A pilot talked into his radio. Little of it made sense to Jeanie, but she was sure information was forwarded to the hospital so they'd know what to prepare for when the helicopter landed.

The part of Jeanie's mind that wasn't occupied with praying marveled at the well-oiled machine of the paramedic team.

The two people working over Michael mostly blocked him from her sight, but once in a while she'd catch a glimpse of Michael's ashen face, streaked with blood. She wanted to ask them to wipe the blood away but kept her mouth shut.

Once she saw Michael's eyes flicker open. They seemed to be clear. Shayla asked him questions, too quietly for Jeanie to hear them over the steady throb of the helicopter's rotors. Michael's deep voice added to the hum of sound and activity.

She did hear Michael say, "Jeanie," once.

The female EMT turned and smiled. "She's here. She's worried sick about you."

Michael's eyes fluttered, and Jeanie could tell he tried to turn. But his head was held steady.

"Just lie still. I told her to stay put in her seat, too. We'll be landing in a few minutes."

Shayla turned to Jeanie. "I'm feeling pretty good about spinal injuries. His fingers and toes are moving fine. We'll do a thorough exam, of course, and we won't remove his neck-stabilizing gear until we're sure. And we have to examine him for internal injuries. If he has any, that could mean surgery."

Jeanie felt tears burn her eyes at the hopeful news.

"He's definitely got a broken arm, and since he was unconscious, he's likely got a concussion. Plus the cut on his head is nasty."

The woman's voice started to sound like it was far away. The little roaring cabin seemed to get darker and her vision tunneled.

Shayla suddenly knelt at Jeanie's side, adjusting her seat belt and shoving Jeanie's head down between her waterlogged knees. Jeanie didn't know why the woman attacked her, but she was too shaky to care.

The next thing Jeanie knew, she was being helped off the air ambulance by Shayla and a stranger, and Michael was rolling away from her with two other attendants.

"What happened?"

"You fainted." Shayla kept an arm around Jeanie's waist, even though Jeanie felt much steadier now, with the helicopter on the ground and hope that Michael would be okay. "We'll leave your clothes with you. Your hands are covered in blood, so once you're steady, you'll need to wash up and change your clothes. The hospital might let you use a shower if you're going to have a long wait."

Jeanie looked and saw crimson fingers. Shayla was right. Dried blood filled every crease and crevice on the front and back of both hands.

Jeanie couldn't think clearly enough to wash up right now, so she found herself settled in a chair in the emergency ward waiting room with a clipboard in her lap and orders to fill out forms. Doing the mundane paperwork kept her from losing her mind while she sat there.

Praying steadily, an hour passed. Then another. Then she found a Bible tucked in a magazine rack. She started reading her strength verses, groping for courage.

Buffy showed up and charged her way across the waiting room to Jeanie's side. Jeanie rose to meet her, and Buffy pulled her into a hug. "Have you heard anything?"

"No, he's with the doctor now."

"Look, this might be him."

The two of them rushed toward the doctor coming from a room down a long corridor. The man glanced down at Jeanie's hands, still coated in blood. "Are you Mrs. Davidson?"

"Yes, how's Michael?"

Buffy put a supporting arm around Jeanie.

"He's going to be all right." The doctor looked exhausted. "We've admitted him for the night. His right humerus is fractured in two locations. He has a mild concussion, but an MRI shows no evidence of a subdural hematoma. The scalp laceration needed suturing. He's got multiple abrasions and contusions, but other than that, he's going to be fine. His fracture requires a pin, so we're prepping him for surgery."

"Surgery?" That was nearly the only thing the man said that made sense.

Buffy tightened her arm around Jeanie's shoulders and whispered, "Broken arm, bump on the head, cuts and bruises, stitches. Nothing serious."

The doctor gave Buffy a tired smile and nodded. "That's exactly right. Broken arm, head bump, cuts, bruises, and stitches. His arm will heal faster with surgery, and your husband assured us he preferred speed. Double fractures are difficult to set under the best circumstances."

"He talked to you?"

"Yes, he was wide awake, answering all our questions rationally. He's going to be fine." The doctor patted Jeanie's shoulder. "The surgery won't take long, but it will be several hours before you can see him. I'll send someone out to let you know when he's done. He needs a night in the hospital, mainly due to the concussion. Barring complications, you'll be able to take him home tomorrow morning."

"Thank you, Doctor."

The man left at a near run. Jeanie wondered who else was in need at this moment.

Buffy sighed. "Wow, I drove over here like a maniac. Bucky phoned and scared me to death. I thought Michael was dying."

Buffy's words were too much, the last straw. "I did, too." Jeanie broke down.

Buffy held her tight and let her cry.

When Jeanie's tears were spent, Buffy said, "We've got to get you cleaned up." Buffy went and said the right thing to the nurse at the ER desk, because she came back with permission for Jeanie to shower. She bullied Jeanie into a downstairs locker room with an unfortunately placed mirror.

Jeanie was shocked to see blood streaking her face and clothes. She'd seen her hands but never noticed the rest. She pulled herself together enough to convince Buffy she could shower and dress without collapsing.

Buffy left to phone Wyatt and let him spread the word that Michael would be okay.

When Buffy returned, Jeanie was dressed and reasonably clean.

Buffy told Jeanie she'd driven Michael's pickup to the hospital and planned to leave it. Wyatt was on his way to take Buffy home. "Now we've got plenty of time for supper. Let's go."

"Supper? What time is it?"

"About five o'clock. Sorry it took me so long to get over here."

"It was morning last time I checked."

Buffy hugged her again. "Can we leave the hospital for supper?"

"No, I want to be here when the surgery is over."

"The doctor said it might be several hours before you could see him. It hasn't been one yet. We've got plenty of time."

"Absolutely not."

"You need a good meal, Jeanie. I'll bet you haven't had a bite to eat since breakfast." Buffy gave her a one-armed hug. "Please, the cafeteria is closed and the vending machines have green sandwiches in them. I might become violent if I have to eat those."

Jeanie laughed and started to feel almost human again. "Well, I don't like getting beaten up, so let's go."

They were back in plenty of time to meet a nurse who had news that Michael was through surgery and waking from the anesthetic.

"Only one person can see him at a time." The nurse gave Buffy a glance.

"I'll go." Jeanie had a flash of irritation so strong she recognized that she was almost irrational. How dare this woman assume Buffy was Michael's wife?

The nurse smiled, the very soul of kindness.

Jeanie got hold of herself. "You might as well go on home, Buff. I'll sit with him tonight."

Buffy pulled a cell phone out of her pocket and handed it to Jeanie. "Phone me if you need anything."

Wyatt chose that moment to come into the waiting room carrying a duffel bag. "Glad Michael's gonna be okay." He gave Jeanie an awkward hug. "I brought him clothes to wear home."

Jeanie nodded and slipped the phone into her pocket. "Thanks, Wyatt. Thanks, both of you. I really appreciate you coming. It helped."

Buffy pulled her close and whispered, "You know I'm not the world's biggest Michael fan."

Jeanie wrinkled her brow in a mock frown. "No, I had no idea."

Buffy smiled. "But I'm glad he's all right."

"Thanks." Jeanie hurried away with the nurse.

At the recovery room door, the nurse turned to block

Jeanie. "I heard you fainted on the chopper."

Jeanie felt her cheeks heat up. "I suppose everybody knows that."

The nurse smiled. "Sure, even your husband. I'm just warning you that there are a lot of tubes and machines, but they're just monitors mainly. We'll unhook them as he fully wakes up. He came through the surgery very well. We've got pain medicine in his IV tube, so he may not make much sense and he may not remember anything tomorrow. So don't worry—or faint—if he's a little. . .weird." The nurse waited.

Jeanie squared her shoulders. "Okay, I'm warned. I'm ready."

nineteen

She wasn't ready.

Michael's face was ashen. His arm was splinted, and a white bandage wrapped his head. Scratches she hadn't noticed before looked red and angry against his pallid face and arms.

She rushed past the nurse to his side.

The tubes and chirping machines seemed to hold him to life.

"Michael!" Her cry, though soft, sounded like grief.

Then his eyes flickered open. "Jeanie? You're here?" His voice was faint and slurred, but he recognized her. He was making sense.

"Of course I'm here, honey."

He fumbled for her hand, his arm held in a rigid cast, his fingers swollen until the skin was shiny.

She gingerly rested her palm under his fingers, afraid she'd hurt him.

The nurse moved to the far side of the bed and made notes on a clipboard as she checked machines. She glanced at Jeanie's nervous attempt to hold Michael's hand. "Good. Be careful. We'll leave an IV in overnight, but the rest of these monitors can come off in about an hour. Then we'll move him to another room for the night. You can come around to this side and sit down. We've got the IV in this hand, so you'll have to be careful no matter what side you're on.

Jeanie turned to focus on Michael and was delighted to see his eyes, still glazed from the sedative but open and watchful. She wondered how bad the concussion was. Maybe he was seeing three of her?

"How about a lil' kiss?"

Jeanie almost laughed. He sounded drunk. And whatever faults Michael had, drinking wasn't one of them. She kissed him. So glad he was alive and with her and in love with her.

The nurse finished her work, and Jeanie rounded the bed.

"Don't leave me!" Michael called, his voice weak but determined.

She had his other hand before he could decide to climb out of bed and come after her. "I'm staying. Don't worry. I just didn't want to bump your broken arm."

"Arm's broken?"

Jeanie ran one finger carefully down his cheek, which was scratched but not deeply. She doubted it would show once he got his color back. She realized he didn't really know much of what was going on. "Yes, you have a broken arm. You're just out of surgery."

She spent the next hour talking with him. Anytime she stopped, he questioned her.

As he became more awake, he began fretting about his bridge, the pieces of it left on the ground. "I should've had help. I shouldn't have been doing it myself. Stupid. Careless."

She began talking again, calming him. "It was an accident. You just slipped."

Michael frowned. "You told me to leave the old people alone. I'd have had some of them there."

"They couldn't have climbed down that creek bank, Michael. You know that. Having them there wouldn't have changed a thing."

"I might not be here. Broken arm. How am I supposed to get those cabins up with a broken arm? I've got reservations for cabins I don't have built."

Jeanie wondered if she'd need to ask the doctor for something to calm him when the door opened and a different nurse bustled in.

"How are we doing?"

Jeanie didn't answer. She wasn't sure how Michael was doing right now, but she knew she felt awful.

He had a mule-stubborn look on his face, as if he were planning to get out of bed and get back to work. "I'm fine. Can I get out of here tonight?"

Jeanie moved aside as the woman studied the machines and asked Michael questions. That seemed to divert him from fretting, and Jeanie breathed a sigh of relief.

By the time the nurse was through, the doctor came by on rounds. Then they moved Michael out of recovery. It was late evening before they were alone again, and either he was exhausted or some medicine had kicked in, because Michael was smiling, heavy-lidded and sweet again.

Jeanie enjoyed the calm, but she knew the storm was coming. She'd have her hands full getting him to lie still long enough to recover.

But for now, he had a sweet, groggy smile on his face, and he whispered love to her as he fell asleep.

Jeanie sat in a recliner next to his bed and dozed fitfully all night.

Michael woke early with some help from nurses checking his blood pressure. As soon as he and Jeanie were alone, he started growling. "Let's get out of here."

"We can't leave until we see the doctor." Dark circles under his eyes worried her. "Are you in pain?"

"Of course I'm in pain," he snapped. The outburst made him drop his head back against his pillow. "My head is killing me. Can you not ask me any stupid questions for a while?"

"Do you need something for the pain?"

"Great, more questions. Go see if the doctor is around so we can get out of here."

Jeanie hesitated, but she forced herself to stand her ground. She caught Michael's uncasted hand. The one with the

IV. "Michael!" She spoke sharply trying to cut through his temper and pain and the remnants of the sedative.

He froze and turned his eyes on her, but despite the rebellious look on his face, he paid attention.

"Honey, stop thrashing around. You'll hurt yourself, and if the doctor doesn't believe you're going to be careful, he might sedate you again and keep you here another day. Now control yourself while I go get the doctor." She watched carefully, afraid he might get up and dress and leave without waiting for the doctor—or her if she was slow. "I'll be back in two seconds. You'd better still be in that bed."

She left, moving at double time because she knew he'd only wait so long.

When she came back, less than a minute later, he was sitting on the side of his bed.

"Oh, Michael. You'll hurt your arm." She rushed forward.

He looked up sheepishly, with a bit of red-cheeked temper showing. "Just help me on with my clothes, okay? I can at least be ready to go when the doctor finally shows up."

"All right, honey. But we're going to go slow. Let's start with your pants. We can't do your shirt until they've taken the IV out."

A nurse came in just as Jeanie helped Michael stand.

"You should be in bed." The nurse drew Jeanie's attention.

"We're being careful."

"When's the doctor going to show up?" Michael barked the question.

Jeanie wished she had a leash—and maybe a muzzle.

The nurse scowled and hurried out.

The doctor showed up only a few minutes later. "You haven't been released yet, Mr. Davidson."

"I know. I'm just getting ready to go as soon as you do release me." But from Michael's tone, Jeanie knew he was leaving.

The doctor seemed to know it, too. He ordered the nurse to remove Michael's IV, and while the nurse worked in quiet disapproval, the doctor signed some papers and wrote out two prescriptions.

"One for pain, one an antibiotic." He issued warnings and instructions that Jeanie tried to pay attention to as Michael headed out the door. "Wait for a wheelchair and for your wife to bring the car around."

Michael was gone.

The doctor shook his head. "He's in a lot of pain, Mrs. Davidson. It's going to make him grouchy."

"You think?" Jeanie rolled her eyes. "I've got to go. He's liable to fall on his face."

She rushed after Michael, glad Buffy had managed to park the truck close to the hospital, because Michael wasn't waiting for her to drive up or for a wheelchair to roll him out.

She got to the door just in time to unlock the passenger's side for her stubborn husband.

He squinted at her.

"Don't even think about saying you'll drive."

With a huff of disgust, he climbed in and sat, leaning back against the seat as if he were in agony. He barked orders at her as she pulled out of the hospital parking lot then threw a minor fit when she pulled into a drugstore drive-through to fill his prescriptions.

"The pain pills make me dizzy. I don't want them."

"Well, what about the antibiotic? If you get an infection in those cuts or that surgical wound, you'll be twice as long healing. The doctor said you can start moving around as soon as possible. We'll hire someone to help with the cabins. You can give orders, just like when you were a contractor. You'll get everything done in time."

Michael gave her a furious look, but he didn't yell. Their gaze held, and to her surprise, Michael looked away first.

"I'm sorry, Jeanie." He put his hand on his head, touching the back and grimacing. "I've got a goose egg back there. My ribs are killing me. The head and rib injuries hurt worse than the broken arm. I'm taking it all out on you. I know that's not fair. I'll probably bite your head off ten times in the next few days. I just feel like my control is really fragile right now. But I'll try and keep things together."

Jeanie's fear ebbed as he spoke. "I'll try and be patient."

"Thanks." Michael shifted to reach for his seat belt and stifled a groan of pain. Jeanie quickly gave the perscription to the woman at the pharmacy drive-thru window. Michael sat in a quiet, cranky pool of a sulk while she got his medicine. With some wheedling, she even managed to get him to take the pills.

He must have felt awful or he'd never have agreed to it.

With a fair amount of backseat driving, they were out of town. And soon Michael was dozing in his seat. Jeanie sighed with relief to have him unconscious.

Not a good sign.

twenty

"Can you get me a refill of coffee?"

Michael snapped his fingers, and Jeanie bit her bottom lip at his crankiness. Poor Michael was hurting terribly. He had insisted on coming to work today. The day after he was released from the hospital. He'd tried to come in yesterday, but Jeanie had refused to bring him, and since the day was half over, she'd prevailed—barely.

Jeanie exchanged a worried glance with Glynna who was cooking up her usual delicious lunch menu, then rushed to Michael with the coffee, afraid he'd get up, serve himself, and then collapse. It was quiet at the Buffalo Café at the moment. The breakfast rush was over; the ten o'clock coffee crowd hadn't arrived. It was one of those rare moments when the café was empty. And it wouldn't last long.

Jeanie ran one hand along Michael's shoulders. "Here you go. Can I get you a cinnamon roll or something?" Maybe a shot of sugar would give him enough energy to keep him from sliding off his chair.

Michael looked up from his laptop, where a bookkeeping program filled the screen. Dark circles underlined his eyes, his complexion too pale. "No."

"We've got plenty of people to fill in the lunch shift, and Glynna can handle things until then. Let me take you home."

"No!"

Jeanie jumped at his sharp tone. She saw Glynna lean down to look out of the kitchen window behind the counter

136

that lined the south side of the dining room, her brow furrowed with worry.

He raised his good hand. His other was strapped to his chest with a sling. "I'm sorry. I just need to get these figures balanced before Jake comes in. He's going to help me find people to finish the work."

"Can you believe they finished the footbridge?" Jeanie looked out of the big front window and saw a beautifully framed view of the rope bridge, now in place across Cold Creek.

Michael caught her hand. "There are great people in this town. You were right about them being generous and me asking too much of them. I threatened Bucky to keep him from forming a cabin-raising party to finish the place while I'm hurt."

"I heard you threaten the man." The sound of a buzz saw droned from near the creek. "You'll notice it didn't work."

"He claims he just wanted to use his new saw. It's his day off, so he's cutting lumber."

"Bucky does love his power tools." Jeanie smiled, refilled Michael's cup, poured one for herself—she was exhausted from being up all night with Michael, who had awakened, moaning in pain, time after time—and then slid into the chair beside her poor battered husband.

Jeanie could hear hammering in the background, and she knew there was more going on than sawing. Michael had to know, too. It only emphasized how exhausted he must be that he didn't go out to watch the proceedings.

"I just need another couple of hours with these books. I'll set up a budget for hiring people—and I'm going to use local labor if at all possible. I'll create cabin blueprints—I was working from notes, but a crew will need the details laid out."

Jeanie sighed. "Jake can handle this. You know it. He

helped with several of the other cabins. If he decides he needs a blueprint—which he won't—he can make one himself."

"Jeanie!" Michael's eyes left his spreadsheet, and he glared at her. A look that years ago would have sent her "Yes, Michael"–ing and "No, Michael"–ing.

But she was made of sterner stuff now.

She also knew he was so tired and hurt that he wasn't fully responsible for his actions.

Glynna came out of the kitchen wiping her hands, her mouth in a tight line. "Is there a problem?"

Jeanie shook her head. "We're fine." She turned back to Michael. "You need two hours, even though you're near collapse? Fine. I'm giving you two hours. That's it. No excuses. After that, if you don't let me take you home to get some rest, I'm calling the ambulance again and having you hauled home strapped to a gurney."

Michael's fury faded to a grin. "Yes, ma'am."

She leaned over and kissed him on the unbandaged side of his forehead. "Good boy."

Michael snickered as he turned back to the figures.

❧

"I've got to get out there, Jeanie. Don't touch my laptop. You'll mess it up. And don't even think of doing the café accounts. It'll take me longer to fix it than if I just do it myself."

"I'll leave it alone, honey." Jeanie came back to the table where Buffy sat next to Emily. Emily cradled her little son in her arms.

Through the window, Jeanie saw Michael waving his good arm. She'd kept him quiet for nearly four days, mostly because he had a wicked headache. Now he couldn't do things himself, but he could order his crew around.

Their wedding day had come and gone without notice—or a wedding. Jeanie had ached when she realized Michael had forgotten to renew their vows but found the energy to oversee the cabin construction.

As Jeanie slid into her chair, Emily looked up from Logan.

Buffy set her coffee cup aside. "What's going on with you and Michael?"

Jeanie straightened, surprised. She hadn't expected this. "Nothing. He's doing great. We're supposed to go to the hospital in Hot Springs Monday and have his stitches out. He might get his cast off, too. The pins and plates in his arm are supposed to work faster than normal healing."

"I don't mean, how is his arm? I mean, why are you letting him talk to you that way?"

"What way?"

"We've been in here for half an hour," Emily said. She had a foundation of common sense that neither Jeanie nor Buffy seemed to possess. Buffy had too many of the same old wounds Jeanie had. But Emily had a great set of parents, dead now, but they'd given her solid values, a clear understanding of God, and a plentiful supply of self-esteem. When Emily had advice, Jeanie listened.

"And?" Jeanie waited.

"And Michael has been barking at you like a junkyard dog." Emily looked at Buffy. "Is this the way he used to treat her?"

Buffy nodded. "How does he have the nerve to talk to you like that? 'Don't touch my laptop. Don't even think of doing the café accounts.' You were doing the accounts for the Golden Days Senior Center for a year before he came dragging himself in here."

"I don't even like bookkeeping." Jeanie smiled. She was so glad Michael was getting better she couldn't help the joy in her heart. She'd nearly lost him. "I know he was a little cranky this morning."

"A little cranky? Wyatt would *never* talk to me that way."

Jeanie patted Buffy's arm. "I'm handling it, okay? He's hurting and frustrated because of his arm, and he hates having to ask for help."

"No, he doesn't," Buffy interrupted. "He's asked everyone in this town to work like dogs since he moved here."

Jeanie plowed on. "Right now he's just a little out of control. But he'll stop barking when he's rested. I remember Wyatt after the buffalo stampeded his ranch. He couldn't speak without shooting fire bolts out of his eyes for weeks."

"That was different. We weren't married. He's never—"

"Buffy, will you just drop it?" Jeanie was startled by her tone. It was a whiny, querulous tone that she hadn't used for years.

Buffy fell silent, too. Their eyes met. Jeanie looked away first.

Logan chose that moment to spit up half of his breakfast.

"I'll get a rag from the kitchen." Jeanie jumped up, glad for an excuse to run.

By the time they'd cleaned things up, Jake came in. "The slave driver is giving us a fifteen-minute coffee break. I'm here to warn you about the stampede."

The coffee crowd outlasted Buffy. Jeanie breathed a sigh of relief when her little sister, who'd always been more grown-up than Jeanie, headed for home.

"Jeanie, don't make the guys wait for a refill." Michael leaned back in his chair, massaging his casted arm.

"I'm sorry." She hurried around to warm up the coffee.

"And can you reset that table Emily and Buffy used so it's ready for lunch?"

It had been thoroughly wiped after Logan's mess, but she hadn't put clean silverware out or replaced the paper placemats advertising Cold Creek. Michael had created them with his desktop publishing software.

She hustled to set the table. Yes, he was barking. But he

had nearly died. Her heart still trembled with fear when she thought of his white face, so still, the blood flowing too fast. The helicopter. The long hours of waiting, praying. All she wanted now was to take care of him, make him happy, be a good wife who met her husband's needs.

The work crew cleared out with a scraping of chairs and thumping boots.

Michael heaved himself to his feet. Jeanie saw him flinch with pain. He was so determined, so strong. And all hers.

God, You gave me a miracle. You showed me how much I cared. I will insist he behave better once he's well, and I'll bet I don't have to. He's just tired and frustrated. Right now I need patience. Thank You for sparing him, Lord.

"Jeanie, stop daydreaming. We've got a lunch crowd that'll be here in a few minutes."

"I'm sorry. I was lost in thought." She considered telling him she'd been lost in prayer, but she didn't want him to think she was chastising him by sounding super religious.

"Yeah, right. You're *thinking.*" He left the room, shutting the door a bit too hard.

As Jeanie watched him head for the cabins, she wished he'd let her bring him a chair outside so he could sit, but she'd offered earlier and he'd been embarrassed by it. She needed to be more sensitive to how he felt.

Glynna came out, her stout body wrapped in a white apron. A large bowl in her hands, she stirred as she talked. "He's a big grouch today."

"He's in pain. He needs time. This isn't the real Michael."

Glynna sniffed as she glared through the window at Michael's back. "A real man doesn't use hurting as an excuse to hurt others. He's from the city though. Must be in touch with his feelings or something. I like a man with a stiff upper lip myself."

Jeanie smiled as she cleared the tables. Before long the lunch crowd came in, and she hustled until nearly two o'clock.

Michael came in for lunch, but he didn't speak to her beyond an occasional sharp remark.

Wanting to insist he go home, she kept her worries to herself. He wouldn't thank her for hovering.

twenty-one

Michael awoke alone, as usual.

Why wouldn't she stay in here with him? They were married.

Yes, they'd missed that dumb recommitment ceremony. But they'd already had a wedding. Another one was just a waste of time. If she loved him, she'd stop playing these stupid games and be his wife again.

He was feeling better. She knew that. She wasn't staying away because of his injuries.

He rolled out of bed. Today he'd get this cast off. As he struggled with his clothes, he wished Jeanie would come in and help him. It stung his pride, but he did need help.

He went out into the kitchen and found her pouring eggs into a sizzling skillet.

"I heard you moving around. Breakfast will be ready in two minutes." She smiled over her shoulder at him. A perky smile that reminded him of when she was just a kid and they'd fallen in love. As she stood in the sunlight of the kitchen window, he noticed her hair glinting in the light. She'd lightened it once, but even so it was a lot darker than it had been at one time. He'd loved the shining blond hair of her youth.

"Your hair bleaches out in the summer, doesn't it?"

Jeanie shrugged. "It used to. I don't spend much time in the sun."

"Since you colored it, I see traces of the girl you used to be. You were so pretty."

"I've let it get so dark. The highlights have faded. I should get it redone."

"No, it's fine. Whatever." He kissed her head.

She used her spatula, lifting the edges of the omelet, then sprinkled cheese on the eggs.

"You used to shred fresh cheese." Michael watched her, wishing they could get this meal eaten so he could get to work. "Remember that aged cheddar you'd buy in the deli?"

Jeanie flipped the omelet, turning the circle into a half moon. She was concentrating hard, which is why she didn't answer for a few long seconds. "We use what we have, Mike. No deli in Cold Creek, so I buy shredded cheese at the grocery store. Don't you like it?"

"Hmm." Michael kissed her cheek this time and slid his good arm around her waist. "It's okay if you can't get the good stuff."

She turned before he got a solid hold.

With her hot cast iron skillet in one hand, Michael had to step back quickly. "Be careful with that." Frowning, he went to the table.

"I'm sorry." She slid the omelet out onto his plate. "Go ahead and eat. I've already had breakfast. I'm going to wash up and walk over to the café."

She began running water in the sink. He liked her to sit down with him, but she was bustling around, ignoring him.

"I'll be done in a second. Give me a few minutes to get ready, and we can ride over together." He ate the omelet. A little dry. Too much cheese. He didn't say it though. He'd learned his lesson about finding fault with his wife.

"I'd rather walk. I like the exercise." She clanked the pan noisily and began scrubbing. Michael tried to ask her questions, but she just scrubbed and gave him noncommittal noises for answers.

"We need to go to Hot Springs this afternoon to get the cast off."

"Do you need me along?"

Of course he didn't *need* her, but he'd have liked the

company. "No, I can handle it."

"If you're sure, I'll stay home." She wiped her hands and went into the bathroom, clicking the door closed.

Michael hurried, but Jeanie was already gone when he'd finished dressing. He passed her, driving, only a block from the café. She glanced up when he slowed down, but she waved him on with a smile that bothered Michael. Not a friendly smile, more polite or forced maybe. What was the matter with her today? As if he didn't have enough problems in his life, now he had a moody wife to deal with.

For a second, thinking of Jeanie as moody reminded him of the old days. She used to do this. Answer in single syllables, find countless excuses to leave the room. He didn't want the old days back.

God, I know I'm impatient. I'm sorry. Once I get this cast off and can go back to work, it'll be better. We'll have the wedding, and Jeanie and I will be together completely.

His prayer made him realize it'd been awhile since he'd prayed. And he and Jeanie hadn't been having their devotion time or counseling sessions. He needed to get back to all of that. Then he pulled up to the construction site and saw the men already hard at work. He'd hired himself a real gung-ho work crew.

They spent the morning getting the framing done for all of the remaining cabins. Michael could help one-handed now.

He didn't see more than a glimpse of Jeanie at coffee or lunch. By the afternoon break, she was gone.

He drove to his doctor's appointment and wished she'd ridden along, because he felt shaky after the cast was off. His elbow, wrist, and shoulder burned like fire. The surgical wounds were tender. His whole arm looked sickly and wrinkled and white. He'd lost muscle mass in just these few weeks, and his right arm looked almost withered in comparison to his other.

The doctor assured him it was normal and the stiffness and pain would fade and the muscles would develop again fast. Still, it would have been nice to have Jeanie fussing over him. She had a gift for comfort.

A servant's heart, Pastor Bert had said. He needed to remember that and not demand too much, because Jeanie would give until she had nothing left. He went into the house, determined to apologize for all the growling he'd been doing, and saw his wife was now almost completely blond.

Diverted from his apology, he reached out his good arm to hug her, but she picked up a stack of mail and didn't notice.

"I like your hair. It's pretty."

"I'm glad you like it. I was a little afraid to let Mamie at In-Hair-It bleach it, but I couldn't drive into Rapid City since you had the truck, so it was her or nothing." She began laying junk mail in one stack and making a pile for him and her. He noticed her mail was skimpy.

"How's your arm?" She didn't even look.

"It hurts like crazy. Stiff—the joints are used to being held still."

A furrow creased her brow, and she looked at him and laid her hand on his wrist. "I'm sorry."

She turned to him enough that he could see her face clearly. "You're wearing makeup, too."

Jeanie smiled and turned back to the mail. "I remember you used to like me to fix myself up a little. I've really let myself go in the last few years."

"Well, why wouldn't you? There was no man around to impress." He tried to flirt with her, coax a smile.

She didn't even look up. Instead, she stared at a sales flyer as if she wanted to memorize the price of sirloin steak.

He flexed his arm and nearly gasped from the pain. Why was Jeanie so moody? Why when he was the one in pain? And he'd just told her she looked nice.

A buzzer went off in the kitchen. "There's supper." She turned away from him without so much as looking in his eyes. In fact, he didn't think they'd made eye contact since he'd come in.

"It'll be ready in a minute. Come on and eat whenever you're ready." She vanished through the kitchen doorway.

His jaw set, annoyed by her strange attitude, Michael flicked through the mail, noting she'd kept several pieces for him that she knew he wouldn't want. What a waste of time to have to sort through it twice.

He went into the kitchen to find she'd grilled a steak. That meant he'd have to cut his meat and that would hurt. Like she even cared.

twenty-two

Michael fought to keep his teeth clenched against the angry words.

Three days without the cast and his whole arm still ached with every move. The August heat was oppressive. The crew worked hard and would make the deadline, but it would be close. He needed those cabins done in time for Labor Day weekend, and that was coming up fast.

God, please make this nuisance of an arm heal. It makes me feel so out of control. I know I'm being a grouch. Help me stop, Lord.

He sat down at the table and saw— "Hamburgers again?" It had been five weeks since his accident. His stitches were out, the cast was off, and his bruises were mostly gone. Only the aches and pains in his arm reminded him of his brush with death.

"Last night I made pork chops. You said a hamburger was the only thing you could eat with one hand. You said to make this."

He got so sick of her "I'm sorry." If she did things right, she wouldn't have to apologize all the time. She slid bread onto the table.

Michael stood up, too afraid to speak to ask Jeanie to get him anything. He got the ketchup and mustard out. He'd need it to choke down another dry burger. She should have known that if she was going to serve him the same garbage every night, he'd need to smother the taste.

He set the condiments on the table and noticed the loaf of bread, still in the plastic bag. Grabbing a small plate out of the cupboard, he put a few slices on and centered it. Nicer.

"Sorry, I'm in pain, okay. I don't mean to pick at you." The pain was definitely easing, but he'd figured out sweet Jeanie would put up with anything if he played the pain card. He picked up his sandwich one-handed, remembering how convenient a burger was. He straightened his silverware but carefully said nothing about the sloppy way she'd set the table.

"You yelled about the ketchup and mustard being messy the last time we had burgers." Jeanie took two slices of the bread and started her own burger.

"It's just hard to eat plain when you let the burger get cold. My fault. That call lasted a lot longer than I expected. I noticed that you left the meat on as long as you could."

Jeanie didn't look up from her plate. "A nice way of saying it's burnt."

"It's fine. Let me tell you about the call."

Jeanie listened but stayed focused on making her sandwich then picked at her food. She always picked, couldn't just sit down to a meal. It irritated him, but he said nothing. He'd found fault with her before. Those days were over. He was a new man.

God help it to become an instinct so I don't have to watch my mouth all the time.

He hit a particularly crunchy part of the burger and left the table to spit it out in the trash. Coming back, he finished telling her about the progress on the cabins.

"I've finally got the Web site done. I'm going to load it tomorrow. I'm hoping it will really bring in the customers."

Jeanie nodded, but Michael had the sense that she wasn't excited. He wanted her to be a full partner in every way. She got up and took her plate to the sink, but his frustration made him rise from the table and pull her away from the dirty dishes.

"Kiss me."

"Let me finish here first, Mike."

He turned her around and was surprised that a smile didn't break out. She was so generous with her smiles. "What is it?"

"I feel like we need to talk, but you're not going to like it. I suppose I could just let it go, but. . ."

"No, what is it? We promised we'd be honest with each other." He drew her firmly back to the table and stood over her until she sat down.

She stared at her hands, folded in her lap, and Michael had a flashback to the many times he'd stared at the top of her bowed head. Her body language reminded him of their marriage as it used to be.

Swallowing hard, he pulled his chair closer to hers and sat. "What is it? Tell me."

She spoke to her hands—an annoying habit, but he didn't mention it. He'd learned to keep all his unkind opinions to himself. He loved her for herself, quirky behavior included.

He wasn't going to pick at her to be better, stronger, a full partner. He understood that she was capable of only so much. Look at the way she'd dropped out of that LPN program. He'd expected her to quit. Jeanie had been a quitter since the time they'd met. When he offered her a way out, she'd grabbed it. Just like she'd grabbed a chance to get out of doing book work for the café. He'd checked her figures when she wasn't looking, and she made too many mistakes. He'd been quietly correcting them, but it took him so long that he might as well be doing the work himself.

"I'm thinking of moving out."

Michael froze. Even his thoughts quit. His mind went blank as her words hit him out of nowhere.

"I don't want to, but I don't think this is working. I spend time every day being scared of your temper."

Then his mind clicked back into place—a bad place. "My temper?" Michael slammed his fist on the table, and she jumped. Well, she ought to jump. He'd been working his heart out controlling his temper, and now she said she was scared?

"I'm not happy, Michael. Things were going pretty well before you were hurt, but even before that you were going back to the old habits of insulting me, finding fault with me. But I was handling it. I was standing up to you, and you were taking it well. But I—I guess my ability to be brave around you has wilted since you've been hurt. I've been working harder and harder to keep *you* happy, but it's *not* because I love you." She looked up, staring him straight in the eye. "I do love you. There's so much about you to love. But. . .maybe it's me. . .maybe the way you act is perfectly normal and I'm the one with the problem. But I'm afraid of you. And I hate that. I hate it that my heart races when I know the hamburgers are a little bit burnt."

"I didn't complain."

"I was already worried before you came in the room. No, you didn't complain, but you were annoyed and fighting to control it. If you think you're good at covering that up, you're not. And you did make wisecracks. You can't quite control that."

"What did I say?"

"I didn't write it down." Jeanie surged to her feet. "I hate the racing heart, the fear, the tension. I remember this from before. The feeling that I should be taking notes, detailing all your insults and slights, because they're usually small, just tiny cuts, none of them so bad by themselves, and yet, by the time you're done, I'm bleeding to death. I annoyed you with supper. I annoy you when I'm not an enthusiastic partner. I just plain annoy you by existing. You think—"

"Jeanie." He stood and his height made it easy for him to look down on her. "I made a point of not saying a single thing even though the meal was cold and burnt. You can't leave me because of things I *didn't* say. The whole point of us working on this marriage is that I've got a—a control-freak problem. I know that. I like everything done just exactly to suit me. But you have your own ways. I'm respecting that. You're just. . .I don't know. . .projecting old feelings onto me. You're remembering what I'd have said before and blaming me for that now. When have I yelled? When have I done anything to scare you?"

"I'm scared of you right now." Jeanie stood and squared her shoulders. "If this were the day after you first came back, I'd call the pastor and make him throw you out."

His lips formed a tight line, and Jeanie took a step back.

That movement made his stomach dive. "Are you afraid I'll hit you?"

"No. You've never been like that. That's not where my fear is rooted. I just. . .I—" She swung her arms wide and turned her back. "It probably *is* my fault. If I had more confidence, maybe I could take your temper and your contempt and shrug it off."

"Contempt? Jeanie, I haven't treated you with contempt. I haven't."

She turned back to him, her arms crossed tight over her chest, her whole body wrapped around itself, cutting him out, saying, "Stay back." She looked up, and he saw the fear, the unhappiness.

"Wh—" Her voice broke. "What are we going to do?"

God, please don't let this dream slip away from me. Help me. Open my eyes to what she needs to get over this baseless fear.

The prayer helped. Michael pulled in a deep breath, letting go of the anger and, yes, his own fear. He had fears, too, that their marriage would be ruined a second time. He reached out his good hand. "Let's pray together."

Their eyes held. The distrust in Jeanie's expression broke his heart. Finally, that kindness, that generosity of spirit he craved and loved and needed as much as he needed air overcame the distrust. She gave him the very best part of herself. The part he'd taken advantage of since the day they'd met.

She took his hand. "Yes, you're right. Instead of saying I was leaving, I should have said, 'We need to pray together.'"

At the end of their prayer, Michael leaned down to kiss her, to really get the marriage back to the footing they'd been on before he'd fallen.

She turned away. "No, Michael. I'm not ready for that yet." She left him to go to her solitary room.

Left him. She hadn't moved out, but hadn't she really left him in her own way?

God, change her heart.

Michael caught himself. He raised both hands to his face, wishing he could wipe the anger and impatience from his mind. That wasn't the right prayer. Or at least not the only prayer he needed.

God, change my *heart.*

twenty-three

I can't change him. I have to accept that. God, help me love him for exactly who he is. Heal this fear in me. Give me courage, strength, wisdom.

He'd been trying; Jeanie had to admit that. But watching Michael try to control his temper was almost as bad as the temper itself, because he was terrible at pretending. Jeanie's heart raced when he walked around with the black cloud overhead.

Buffy came in to have coffee at the café almost every day. Jeanie felt a new closeness to her little sister, but the fly in the ointment was the way Buffy scowled at Michael and Michael's refusal to sign those papers. The time was nearly gone; Sally would be Buffy's soon.

"I don't know why you have to hassle Michael. He just hates the thought of signing his name to that paper, but he's not going to do anything to stop the adoption."

"You don't know that. You said he refuses to talk about it."

Jeanie had said that. And it was probably true. But honestly, she'd never pushed him, never even brought it up. She dreaded imagining how he'd fly off the handle, maybe do something rash like protest the adoption.

If they were just quiet and let the deadline come and go, everything would be fine.

Michael brought the men in as he always did for morning coffee break, and Jeanie spent the fifteen minutes jumping and waiting on them all before Michael could snap at her. He was trying. Since she'd threatened to leave him, she could tell he was trying.

When they left, Jeanie sank back down beside Buffy at the table nearest the front window. They could look out at the trees lining the creek and the mountain peaks that soared behind them. The neat cabins were nearly done. Tourists were staying in nearly all of the finished buildings.

The café phone rang, and Jeanie went to get it just as Emily came into view through the window. Stephie was with her, but the little girl ran off. She had a lot of friends in town, so she was no doubt going visiting.

Jeanie listened, tears burning her eyes. Grieving, she hung up the phone.

Emily looked up and was on her feet immediately. "What's wrong?"

Buffy came to Jeanie's side right behind Emily.

"The nursing home called. Janet Lessman died."

Buffy rubbed Jeanie's back. "She'd been doing badly for a while, hadn't she?"

"She was my last remaining hospice patient. I hadn't realized the end was so imminent. I failed that sweet lady and the whole Lessman family when they needed me most."

Emily and Buffy hugged her.

Jeanie dabbed at her eyes and looked up to catch a strange, serious look pass between her sister and her best friend.

"And why do you think you failed them?" Emily guided Jeanie toward the table.

"Because I did. I haven't really been in to see her since. . ." Jeanie couldn't say it.

Buffy had no trouble. "Since Michael came back."

Emily said, "Jeanie, we have to talk."

&

"Mike, we have to talk."

Michael looked away from the door he'd just finished hanging on the last cabin. "Sure, Jake, what is it?"

"Take a walk, okay?" Jake's eyes went to the other men

working nearby. "Its private."

Wondering what was up, Michael swung the door shut and heard the latch click shut solidly. Perfect. With a satisfied smile, he turned and walked along with Jake. "What's up?"

Jake didn't speak until they'd put quite a bit of distance between themselves and the carpenters. Some problem must have come up on the cabins. Michael was a great problem solver, so he prepared to hear about it and fix it.

As they reached the far side of the café that contained the bait and tackle shop, which didn't open for a while yet, Jake stopped, his arms crossed. "What's going on with you and Jeanie?"

That came out of left field. Michael shook his head a little to shift gears from work. "Nothing's going on. Why?"

"Emily and Buffy are in the café right now talking to her. We're really worried. She's changed. When you first came back, after the rugged beginning you two had, it looked like things were going well. But not anymore. She's not happy. And neither are you, Mike."

Michael had focused on Jake. Now he saw Pastor Bert had joined them. From the serious expression on both men's faces, Michael knew they'd planned this.

twenty-four

"We've barely spoken in the last weeks, Jeanie." Emily patted Logan on the back. "We used to talk all the time. Now we barely say hello at church."

"You've been busy."

"I've been almost housebound with a new baby and an overprotective husband. Why haven't you come out to visit?"

"I—I was going to. Then Michael got hurt and—"

"And the gift you sent—you ordered it online, didn't you?"

Jeanie shook her head to clear it. "You didn't like the gift Michael and I gave you?"

"I loved it. That's not the point. You didn't go shopping. You didn't come to visit."

"And you didn't help the Lessman family," Buffy added.

"I feel terrible about that." Hurt crept up along with anger at this strange conversation. "And shopping isn't worth the effort when Michael's so busy."

"What does that have to do with anything? You don't need Michael to buy a present."

"It's not worth—" Jeanie stopped before she admitted it wasn't worth putting up with Michael's scorn if she went to the city alone. Or putting up with his scorn if he had to drive her. She'd had the present overnighted, and she'd put up with his scorn for how much shipping cost.

Jeanie's jaw tightened.

"The thing is—," Buffy began.

Jeanie put up her hand. "I get it now. This is about Michael."

"This is about us loving you, Jeanie." Buffy said. "And we want you and Michael to be happy. And you're not." Silence stretched between the three women.

Jeanie thought of a dozen things to say, all full of defending herself and excusing Michael. Finally, she thought it through to the end and knew. "You're right." Why had Jeanie let it happen? Because she had. Michael had been a tyrant, but Jeanie had put up with it, almost without a whimper. "All the little cuts. Even if every little insult is true and he acts like he's trying to protect me and help poor, dumb little me, it's still wrong."

"Jeanie, you're not dumb. Stop." Emily rested her hand on Jeanie's arm, and Jeanie realized that the two of them were facing her, almost as if they intended to hold her prisoner here until she admitted they were right.

Well, they wouldn't have long to wait. "You're right. I'm not dumb. I can drive in Rapid City. I was getting top grades in my LPN class. I'm not incompetent. He's not protecting me. He's cutting me off from my friends and my family and making me dependent on only him."

Some of the creases eased from Buffy's face, worry replaced by hope. "How can we help you?"

Jeanie ran her hand through her ridiculously blond hair. She realized she had heavy makeup on and a dress and high heels. And her heart was a mess—soiled, angry, and afraid all the time. All the surface changes had changed her inside for the worse. But no more. "Maybe you could help me find my bat."

twenty-five

"What's this about?"

The look in Pastor Bert's eyes sent an odd chill of fear up Michael's spine.

"This is about the pathetic mess you are making of your marriage." Pastor Bert squared off in front of Michael, Jake at his side. "You need to come to grips with what you're doing to Jeanie."

"Is this some kind of. . .joke?" Michael asked, thrown by this sudden confrontational situation.

"No." Jake's eyes warmed with concern. "We care about you and Jeanie. We want you to be happy. At first you seemed to be working things out, but lately things have gone wrong."

Pastor Bert nodded. "I watched Jeanie change since you've been back."

"And I've worked with you enough to know all the gifts you have. I respect your talents and intelligence. Your faith, too," Jake added.

"We're just fine. I appreciate your concern." Michael shook his head. The word *denial* crept into his thoughts.

"I've seen you change just in the few months since you've been in Cold Creek." Jake stood shoulder-to-shoulder with the pastor, his expression grim. "Not so much at work as with Jeanie. You've started being unkind, hurting her."

"No, I haven't. We've worked through our problems. We're happy now. We're in counseling and—"

Pastor Bert cut him off. "You're not in counseling to my knowledge."

"We meet weekly with you."

"Past tense. I haven't seen you for far too long. But I have seen Jeanie give up all her work of service to Cold Creek."

"She was doing too much. She isn't available for everyone to take advantage of anymore." Michael had saved her from that life of endless demands.

"That work meant a lot to her." Pastor Bert looked straight into Michael's eyes. "And you've cut her off from that and made her into a quiet, isolated shadow of her former self."

Michael's heart sank at the pastor's unflinching stare. This was a man he respected, and he'd thought Bert respected him. Bristling, Michael scowled, ready to throw this all back at them. He'd go somewhere else then, to a town that would appreciate all he could do for them. There were people who'd be grateful.

The door to the café slammed open, and Jeanie came out flanked by Buffy and Emily. From the intent look on his wife's face, Michael knew she'd been getting this same kind of scolding he had.

Jeanie moved so she stood between the other men and Michael. She'd tell them. She'd make sure they knew this wasn't appreciated. She'd take his side and—

She turned to face him. Somehow she was standing with them, against him. Emily and Buffy added themselves to the lineup confronting him.

Except Jeanie's expression wasn't confrontational; it was kind. She reached forward and took his hands. Her eyes, so blue, so sweet, were looking at him like. . .like she felt sorry for him.

"When you first came back, we heard what Pastor Bert had to say, and we made a commitment to change, but we're not living up to our commitment. And that's my fault."

Feeling a little less stunned, Michael tried to listen, tried to ignore this ridiculous business and just give Jeanie all the help she needed.

"It's my fault because I've been letting you hurt me, Mike."

"Hurt you?"

"Yes, and whether that's my problem, left over from childhood, or your problem because you need to control me, I still shouldn't have put up with it. I've swallowed all the little cuts, the slights, the insults."

"Like what? What have I ever said to you that wasn't kind?"

Jeanie glanced over her shoulder at Pastor Bert, who now stood behind her in a row with Buffy, Emily, and Jake, standing like guard dogs protecting her from the man who was supposed to love her as Christ loved the church.

Michael felt deeply and shockingly and painfully alone.

Jeanie reached into her pocket. "This isn't scriptural. What's the verse, Pastor Bert? About not keeping track of when people sin against you."

Bert smiled. "It's from the Love Chapter, 1 Corinthians 13. 'Love does not keep track of other people's wrongs.'"

Jeanie held up a roll of paper that looked like it had been torn off a cash register receipt roll, and shook it.

Michael's eyes followed it as it unrolled two feet.

"Then I haven't been loving you biblically, Mike. Because I've been keeping a record of your wrongs—the things you say that make me feel bad."

Michael felt his ears heat up. This was humiliating. He hated this. The heat in his ears turned to heat in his temper.

"Stop." Pastor Bert stepped up beside Jeanie.

"Good. I'm glad you stopped her. She shouldn't discuss something private in front of a group." Michael truly respected and cared for this man. He had a fatherly way about him that Michael never had from his own dad. His dad was a tyrant who could wound everyone with a single word. Michael mentally stumbled over that thought. A tyrant? Was that what these people were accusing him of being?

Bert rested one large hand on Michael's shoulder. "I'm not stopping *her*. I'm stopping *you*. I can see you growing angry. The whole purpose of this gathering is that we all love you."

Michael looked from face to face. He wondered about it.

Pastor Bert might love him; he was a man of God.

Jeanie's eyes said that she loved him, even though she stood there holding a list of his sins.

Emily and Jake, maybe—sure, why not? Jake had worked beside Michael a lot. They were good friends.

Buffy, well, she'd always been a woman of faith. If anyone could love an undeserving brother, it was Buffy.

Michael noticed Wyatt wasn't here. Possibly the man had to work. But Wyatt was the one who'd done the most scowling over those adoption papers. More likely, Wyatt was forbidden to be here because, when they'd planned this, Wyatt had voted to round up a posse, a noose, and a lone oak tree. But these folks mostly did love him—in Christian brotherhood. Yes, even Wyatt might claim that, under threat of torture.

Michael could say that, too. He loved them all right back. And he *was* a tyrant. He could take this intervention like a man. He needed it. He needed them all, a lot more than they needed him.

Nodding, he looked at Jeanie. "Tell me. I'm ready to listen. But before you start, I want you to know you're right. I knew when I first got back here that I was the one with the problems, not you. But I let that get away from me." Michael took her hands. "I need help to change. I let the counseling slide and the daily devotions. I'm sorry."

Jeanie crushed the list in one hand and wrapped her arms

around him. "I love you. And you're not the only one who went wrong."

Brushing her hair back off of her forehead, Michael noticed it was white blond. Her makeup was heavy. Her clothes were too tight. This was his fault. "You've gone wrong by putting away that bat."

Jeanie lifted her chin and smiled. "I've gone wrong because I kept everything inside. You asked me from the start to make you accountable. I failed. I was doing okay until you got hurt, and then I was just so glad you were alive." She hugged him so hard it hurt.

The best hurt Michael had ever felt.

"I was so glad I had you in my life. You were hurt and understandably grouchy, and I wanted to make your life as comfortable as possible. I started saying yes to every demand and. . .I just let it get away from me. It's so much easier to keep quiet, to avoid confrontation, to take all the blame and try to change myself."

"Twist yourself into a pretzel, you mean."

Jeanie shrugged.

"The accident made it worse, Jeanie," Emily said. "But you remember the day Buffy and I heard Michael putting you down. You were already making excuses for him."

Michael realized he couldn't even remember a time he'd insulted Jeanie in front of Emily. It was too easy to let emotionally abusive language slip free. "I think you'd better read me that list."

"I will, but later. When we're alone. And I'll get another bat."

Pastor Bert produced one from the inside pocket of his suit jacket, and Jeanie let go of Michael to take possession.

"Thanks a lot," Michael said dryly.

"And your counseling resumes tomorrow morning. We'll

meet faithfully once a week, and you'd better not make me hunt you down." Pastor Bert sounded kind and unmovable. "You've made promises before, Michael. I really don't know if you can control yourself without someone a little tougher than Jeanie watching you."

"I've stayed too far back from this, too, Michael. I'm not leaving Jeanie to handle you alone." Buffy put an arm across Jeanie's shoulders. "And I tried to talk to you a couple of times about the way Michael treated you, Jeanie, but I let you persuade me to drop it. I won't do that again. If that makes me a meddling little sister, too bad."

They were right. Michael had learned it all at his father's knee, and being a tyrant wasn't something he could change in a day no matter how completely he admitted he had a problem.

Michael looked at the people in front of him, willing to confront him in Christian love, and it struck him that this was what a family meant. This support, this intermingling of lives. And when he thought of it like that, he also knew his whole definition of family had been warped.

He remembered Jeanie's life verse: *"We want you to be very strong, in keeping with his glorious power. We want you to be patient. Never give up. Be joyful."* Jeanie had said she clung to the part about strength but couldn't ever find the joy. He knew now how she felt.

"I want to take my wife home and talk things out." He looked from face to face, until finally he got to the only one that mattered.

Jeanie, her eyes spilling over with tears of pain and love, nodded. "Let's go home."

"Thank you all. I'm going to be a better man."

Jeanie swiped her wrist across her eyes. "I'm going to make sure you are."

"Stop." Buffy's sharp command stopped Michael in his tra[...]

"Before you walk away, we're going to talk about Sally. I've [...] that slide, too. I've talked with Jeanie, but I've never faced yo[...] with this. Are you planning to sign those papers or not?"

Jeanie's arm tightened around Michael.

Silence reigned.

Buffy didn't budge. Neither did the pastor or Jake or Emily.

As the silence stretched, Michael felt pain growing until it ached like a broken arm. He heard echoes from his past. Jeanie scared of him. A baby crying. His own cruelty.

God, I was so steeped in sin. I still am.

The pain deepened as Michael faced all that his choices had cost Jeanie, Sally, and himself. And all the pain the wrong choice now could bring.

"I. . .I don't know if I can, Buffy." The least he could do was be completely honest. It was long past the time for not being completely honest. "I haven't signed them because. . .because I would have to admit I'd failed. To sign my daughter away is—" Michael's voice broke. He whirled away, shocked and humiliated by his lack of control.

Jeanie wrapped her arms tightly around him, and he pulled her hard against him, feeling like a fool for crying. A lifetime of sin crushed him. He'd never taken the time to love Sally as she deserved. He'd given no thought to Jeanie when he'd stormed out of her life.

Michael thought of the Love Chapter. Love is patient, and he was terribly impatient.

Love is kind, and he'd been so unkind to Jeanie and his little girl.

It does not envy. Michael never stopped wanting more, wanting what someone else had.

It does not boast, is not proud. Michael wore his pride like a royal robe, and he never stopped boasting about his success.

is not rude. It is not self-seeking. It is not easily angered.
keeps no record of wrongs.

Michael looked at that list crumpled in Jeanie's hands. But wasn't he the one who had always kept a record of wrongs? Wasn't he the one who had always found fault, never let a chance slip by to criticize?

But he remembered more than the list that convicted him.

He looked into Jeanie's kind eyes, so much more than he deserved. "Love always protects, always trusts, always hopes. It never gives up."

"The Love Chapter," Pastor Bert said quietly.

"I've failed in all of that, Jeanie." Michael's eyes fell shut. It was almost more than he could do to speak the words aloud. "But I'm not going to fail Sally now."

"Michael, please." Fear widened Jeanie's eyes. "You've got to—"

"I mean," he cut her off—and promised himself and God it was for the last time. But this once, because she misunderstood, he stopped her before her hurt could go any deeper. "I mean I'm going to let her go."

Tears burned at his eyes again. But this time he didn't even feel embarrassed. If a man couldn't cry when he gave his child away, then God had no reason to invent tears.

Jeanie threw herself hard against him, buried her face against his chest, and together, for all the failure, all their rugged past, they cried.

A quick signature. Painful as the slash of a knife, but Michael didn't know if it would ever heal. Then he pulled Jeanie close and they turned to go.

Buffy rushed past them to plant herself in their path. "I'm going to be watching you." Her words were tough, but there was kindness in her eyes along with hope. She wanted her sister to be happy. Her expression said she thought that maybe Michael was up to being part of that happiness.

Michael realized he had a real family—a sister, a
in Wyatt, nieces, nephews. . .a wife. True friends, t.
who cared enough to stand in his path when he was hea
down the wrong one, in Jake and Emily. He ran a quick ha
across his eyes to wipe away the tears then leaned down an
kissed Buffy on the cheek. "I'm counting on it."

Buffy stepped aside, and Michael and Jeanie headed for
home to begin again for the last time.

twenty-six

Pastor Bert refused to perform the wedding ceremony until Jeanie and Michael went through intensive counseling.

Even Jeanie was impatient by the time the stubborn man finally agreed, declaring the counseling would continue whether they wanted it or not.

Jeanie wanted it. She was delighted that Michael agreed with her.

Impatience aside, Jeanie loved every minute of those months. She and Michael were talking as they never had before. Michael wasn't always perfect, but he'd learned to catch his temper, recognize it, and calm down, usually before she threatened him with her support system. The bat sat as a reminder, but Jeanie knew they couldn't rely on that alone again.

She went back to her job at the library. Michael now ran the cash register at the mini-mart every other Saturday. The new cabins lined the creek, the restaurant hummed with activity, and Michael agreed it was enough. No more grand plans—just a lovely little vacation spot.

Jeanie dragged Michael into every volunteer project that came her way. They were so busy they had to schedule the wedding on a weekday night, right after choir practice.

It didn't matter; the wedding was small. Buffy and Emily as bridesmaids. Wyatt and Jake as groomsmen. Their children and a very few others as guests—unless they counted that the whole town of Cold Creek came.

But it wasn't as if they were invited. Having a wedding under the beautiful fall foliage out in front of a row of cabins—well, that was public land. Anyone who wanted could stop and stare. Even a few renters quit their vacationing and attended.

Even knowing it was a huge mistake, Pastor Bert insisted Jeanie use the bat as a ring pillow. With Colt and Cody as ring bearers, the rings had no chance of survival. Jeanie suggested tying fake rings on the bat. Michael agreed and kept the real ones in his pocket.

Sally was the flower girl. As she stood beside the pastor, Jeanie realized they hadn't lost their baby. They could love her wholeheartedly without tearing her secure life apart. And wasn't that *real* love?

"Dearly beloved"—Pastor Bert ducked a line drive like he'd played in the majors—"we are gathered here today. . ."

Wyatt had even warmed up to Michael enough that he acted as best man—and referee. When his Stetson went flying off of his head, Wyatt finally grabbed the bat away from both boys then growled under his breath at the pastor, "I can keep 'em occupied, but I can't keep 'em quiet. Hurry it up."

The vows were spoken quickly. But Jeanie heard the sincerity in every word Michael spoke, and she poured all her love into her own promises.

As the pastor pronounced them man and wife, he closed with an unlikely wedding scripture: "'We want you to be very strong, in keeping with his glorious power. We want you to be patient. Never give up. Be joyful.'"

It was finally, completely true. Jeanie smiled at Michael and knew joy. A joy that hadn't been there when they'd married the first time. And it hadn't been there when he came back. It had been a rocky road, but God knew they'd needed to walk such a broken path to learn true strength, to find abiding patience, to experience great joy, to know true love.

As the scripture said, they'd never given up. And they'd made it.

Smiling, Jeanie stood on her tiptoes, eager to obey the pastor when he told her bossy bridegroom to kiss the bride.

A Letter To Our Readers

Dear Reader:

In order that we might better contribute to your reading enjoyment, we would appreciate your taking a few minutes to respond to the following questions. We welcome your comments and read each form and letter we receive. When completed, please return to the following:

Fiction Editor
Heartsong Presents
PO Box 719
Uhrichsville, Ohio 44683

1. Did you enjoy reading *The Bossy Bridegroom* by Mary Connealy?
   ❏ Very much! I would like to see more books by this author!
   ❏ Moderately. I would have enjoyed it more if

   _____

   _____

   _____

2. Are you a member of **Heartsong Presents**? ❏ Yes ❏ No
   If no, where did you purchase this book? _____

   _____

3. How would you rate, on a scale from 1 (poor) to 5 (superior), the cover design? _____

4. On a scale from 1 (poor) to 10 (superior), please rate the following elements.

   ____ Heroine   ____ Plot
   ____ Hero   ____ Inspirational theme
   ____ Setting   ____ Secondary characters

. These characters were special because? _____

_____

_____

6. How has this book inspired your life? _____

_____

_____

7. What settings would you like to see covered in future
   Heartsong Presents books? _____

_____

_____

8. What are some inspirational themes you would like to see
   treated in future books? _____

_____

_____

9. Would you be interested in reading other **Heartsong
   Presents** titles? ❏ Yes ❏ No

10. Please check your age range:
     ❏ Under 18   ❏ 18-24
     ❏ 25-34   ❏ 35-45
     ❏ 46-55   ❏ Over 55

Name _____

Occupation _____

Address _____

City, State, Zip _____

A ll aboard! Next stop—
Texas, where love derails
the best-laid plans of
a reluctant rancher, a
meddlesome schoolmarm,
and two children on an
orphan train.

Historical, paperback, 288 pages, 5³⁄₁₆" x 8"

Please send me ____ copies of *Gingham Mountain.* I am enclosing $10.97 for each.
(Please add $4.00 to cover postage and handling per order. OH add 7% tax.
If outside the U.S. please call 740-922-7280 for shipping charges.)

Name_____

Address _____

City, State, Zip _____

Presents

Great Inspirational Romance at a Great Price!

Heartsong Presents books are inspirational romances in
contemporary and historical settings, designed to give you an
enjoyable, spirit-lifting reading experience. You can choose
wonderfully written titles from some of today's best authors like
Wanda E. Brunstetter, Mary Connealy, Susan Page Davis,
Cathy Marie Hake, Joyce Livingston, and many others.

When ordering quantities less than twelve, above titles are $2.97 each.
Not all titles may be available at time of order.

HEARTSONG
P R E S E N T S

If you love Christian romance...

$10.⁹⁹

You'll love Heartsong Presents' inspiring and faith-filled romances by today's very best Christian authors...Wanda E. Brunstetter, Mary Connealy, Susan Page Davis, Cathy Marie Hake, and Joyce Livingston, to mention a few!

When you join Heartsong Presents, you'll enjoy four brand-new, mass market, 176-page books—two contemporary and two historical—that will build you up in your faith when you discover God's role in every relationship you read about!

Mass Market 176 Pages

Imagine...four new romances every four weeks—with men and women like you who long to meet the one God has chosen as the love of their lives...all for the low price of $10.99 postpaid.

To join, simply visit www.heartsong presents.com or complete the coupon below and mail it to the address provided.

✂ -

YES! Sign me up for Heart♥ng!

NEW MEMBERSHIPS WILL BE SHIPPED IMMEDIATELY!
Send no money now. We'll bill you only $10.99 postpaid with your first shipment of four books. Or for faster action, call 1-740-922-7280.

NAME_____

ADDRESS_____

CITY_____ STATE _____ ZIP _____

MAIL TO: HEARTSONG PRESENTS, P.O. Box 721, Uhrichsville, Ohio 44683
or sign up at **WWW.HEARTSONGPRESENTS.COM**